Entwined Publishing books by Haylynn Downing

The Cursed Rose
A Rose Among Beasts
A Rose in Darkness
A Rose Ever Altered

I0527717

The Cursed Rose

A ROSE EVER ALTERED

HAYLYNN DOWNING

ENTWINED PUBLISHING

A Rose Ever Altered
ISBN # 978-1-80250-262-6
©Copyright Haylynn Downing 2025
Cover Art by Kelly Martin ©Copyright August 2025
Interior text design by Entwined Publishing
Published by Eclipse, an Entwined Publishing imprint

This is a work of fiction. All characters, places and events are from the author's imagination and should not be confused with fact. Any resemblance to persons, living or dead, events or places is purely coincidental.

All rights reserved. No part of this book may be used, reproduced, or distributed in any form or by any means, including but not limited to electronic, mechanical, photocopying, recording, or by any information storage and retrieval system, without prior written permission from the publisher. This book and its contents are expressly reserved from use in training artificial intelligence technologies or systems. Furthermore, this work is expressly reserved from the text and data mining exception, in accordance with Directive (EU) 2019/790 of the European Parliament and of the Council.

Applications should be addressed in the first instance, in writing, to Entwined Publishing. Unauthorised or restricted acts in relation to this publication may result in civil proceedings and/or criminal prosecution.

The author and illustrator have asserted their respective rights under the Copyright Designs and Patents Acts 1988 (as amended) to be identified as the author of this book and illustrator of the artwork.

Published in 2025 by Entwined Publishing, United Kingdom.

Entwined Publishing is a division of Totally Entwined Group Limited.

A ROSE EVER ALTERED

Dedication

To all the readers who have followed Brielle and
the Grimm Brothers from the beginning.
Thank you.

Chapter One

Xander

Screaming.

The sound echoes through the room around me, but I don't flinch, my face a blank, uncaring slate.

Beast.

"Please, stop," the woman begs.

Her words are a sharp, shrill screech that breaks through my carefully tailored mask. My eye twitches.

Be a Beast.

The snap of the leather registers before the sting of it tears into my flesh. The blow is sudden and intense enough to knock me to my knees.

"No emotions!" my father barks over the crack of another blow, the pain of his belt ripping into my skin punctuating his demand.

Be a Beast.

I bite back a cry of pain as another blow lands between my shoulder blades, knowing all too well that the sight of any weaknesses will only prolong my punishment. *And her torture.*

"I-I swear, I didn't know."

It's not the first time the woman has pled her innocence. She hasn't realized — between the blows to her head and the murder of her husband — that it doesn't really *matter* if she knew about his transgressions. She's a lesson.

"You're a liar." My father's split attention doesn't allow me a moment of reprieve.

He brings the belt down against my back again before turning it on the woman. She screams as the buckle splits open her cheek, but this time, I don't flinch. I swallow my emotions — the rage, the pain, and the fear.

I'm a Beast.

Nothing more. Never anything more.

"P-please..." Her cries are weaker now as blood pools down her mangled face, staining her torso a haunting shade of red.

My father moves from me to stalk his target, his footsteps heavy on the cement beneath them. Her head drops forward in defeat, her shoulders slumping as she finally realizes something I learned long ago. *My father shows mercy to no one.*

"Are you watching, Beast?" He glances at me over his shoulder and latches onto the woman's chin.

He forces her head back so her eyes find mine across the room, and yanks his gun free of its holster. I can almost taste her fear as I swallow the lump that's formed in my throat.

I have to be a Beast.

"Yes, Father."

* * * *

The woman's cries and the guttural sounds of her death follow me as I come out of the nightmare. Even lying here half awake, hovering the lines of awareness and oblivion, I *still* hear her.

Those screams…

They're real.

It's real, and it's Brielle.

I bolt upright — the sudden movement rousing Everett — and dart toward the door. "Get security. Find Rhys. Now!"

Brielle's screams are echoing from somewhere down the hall, and they continue to reverberate through my skull long after they've ended. They're engraved there, stirring panic in my gut with each thump of my racing heart.

"Brielle!?" I shout. Silence settles in the hall and my anxiety skyrockets. "Amour!?"

I turn wildly, a feral roar ripping from my throat as I eye each closed door, rage burning through my veins. *I fell asleep.* How the fuck did I fall asleep?

"Brielle!?" I start banging on doors, my ears straining as I listen desperately for a sound, a sign, or *anything* that might point me in her direction. "Brielle, where are you!?"

People are filing into the hall, their curiosity stoked by the commotion I'm causing as I continue my rushed path down the hall. They're murmuring, hissing questions and accusations to one another, their voices in the shallow space stoking my rage.

"Shut the fuck up!" My panic-fueled demand quiets the crowd.

Panting, I shove past the bystanders who have blocked the hall, and continue rapping on closed doors until finally, in the silence, I hear her.

Muffled cries come from behind the one in front of me, the sound of her distress coiling fear deep in the pit of my stomach.

"Brielle?" I yank on the handle, but it's locked, only worsening my panic. "Amour, can you hear me? Can you open the door?"

I press an ear against the wood, trying unsuccessfully to assess the situation on the other side. Is she alone? Is someone with her? Is she hurt? Is she *being* hurt?

That last thought has me stepping back. Drawing my leg up, I swing it forward and boot the door just below the knob with as much force as I can pack behind the blow. It should be enough to kick it in, but the door only shakes in its frame. *Fuck.*

I kick it again.

And again.

And again.

I lift my foot, preparing to deliver a fifth blow, when a faint *click* resonates from the other side of the door. I stall, breath caught in my throat, and watch with wide eyes as the door cracks open. I inch forward, unsure what to expect, and all but catch Brielle as she collapses through the doorway with a loud sob.

"Amour." I bury my nose in her hair and race my hands along her body, searching for injuries.

She's on the verge of hyperventilating, her breaths coming in short, rushed gasps, but she seems physically fine. I don't understand the cause of her panic until my eyes slide to the ajar door behind her, and glimpse the man hanging in it.

Lincoln Fisher.

Fuck.

"Clear out. Everyone, move!" Everett has returned.

Rhys and Joe are hot on his heels, and together, they usher away the hovering crowd, their booming demands scattering the vultures.

"I've got you, Amour. It's okay, just breathe." I stroke a hand through her waves and tuck her into my chest.

"Secure the level and lock down the building. No one leaves until they've been cleared, understood?" Everett has taken control, and Joe is quick to follow his orders.

A month ago, it would have pissed me off to see Everett taking the lead and ordering around *my* hired men. Now, I'm fucking *grateful* for it as I tug Brielle back a step so my brothers can access the room. I don't go with them. I can see enough from here to grasp what's happened.

Lincoln got greedy.

"Xander." Brielle's small voice pulls my attention down as her fingers dig into the fabric of my shirt. "Take me home. Please, I want to go home."

At first, I think she's asking to go to the house I stole her from, but when her wet eyes lift to meet mine, I understand.

She wants *our* home.

"Brass. Blaze." I call over her head, ensuring she stays turned away from the scene behind her. "I'm getting her out of here."

Rhys' green orbs find me across the room, and his brow furrows as he glances between me and the trembling woman in my arms. I can decipher his concern and the silent order that follows me as I lead her down the hall. *Take care of her.*

I band an arm around her waist and move my thumb in small circles at her hip as we approach the elevator.

"I'd just wanted to get cleaned up. I-I didn't think…" I'm not sure the whispered words are meant for me, but I shush her anyway.

"It's okay, Brielle. Slow, deep breaths. In and out," I coax.

Her teeth chatter uncontrollably, and I can see her entire body riddled with goosebumps as I gently pull her into the elevator. She's shaking, and although she mirrors my deep breathing, I'm not sure she's truly seeing me.

This isn't an outcome we anticipated. I'm not sure how the son of a bitch got through these doors, or how he managed to die right under our fucking noses, but I intend to find out.

Once Brielle is safe.

When the elevator doors open on the first floor, I stoop down and scoop Brielle into my arms. There's a crowd of patrons gathered near the front entrance, and I quickly carry her through the foyer before their raised voices can reach us. Rumors are spinning, and I will not have our girl caught in the middle.

With easy strides, I cross the parking lot toward the waiting car. Only one man has been left behind with the vehicle, and I growl at him as I open her door.

"Take us home."

Chapter Two

Everett

"Brass. There's something you need to see."

Joe stands just inside the room, a frown deepening the wrinkles already carved around his thin lips. He's eyeing Lincoln's body, which Rhys and I have just freed from the rope tethering it to the ceiling.

"What did you find?" Rhys questions, beckoning the man forward with a wave of his hand.

Neither of us looks up from the dead man that lies between us. Lincoln's tongue is *missing*, a gory message in this fucked puzzle we're trying hard to decipher. It wasn't clean, the man's murder, or the severing of his tongue. Blood litters the floor, and has soaked down the front of his body. He was still alive when he was cut — if the blood loss is any indication — a realization that pleases me, despite it having been someone else's hand to have dealt that pain. We all wanted to kill him ourselves. The fucker who haunts and will *continue* haunting Brielle's dreams, even now, after his death.

Joe holds up a video on his cell, a shitty capture of the surveillance feed. I peel my eyes away from Lincoln and snatch the phone. Hitting play, I watch as Brielle appears in the corner of the screen, obviously distracted. She's just left the locker room, and a man is heading in her direction. The suit he's wearing looks expensive, even in this grainy video, and his salt-and-pepper hair is neat beneath the strap of his mask.

"That's gotta be Lincoln's boss, right?" Rhys asks.

I don't respond, my jaw clenching as the man steps in front of Brielle, blocking the path back to our room.

"I don't understand. If this is him, he had his chance. Why didn't he—" I break off abruptly as the fucker begins circling her.

If he says anything to her, our cameras don't pick it up, and I curse when I notice the full-face mask concealing his identity from us. He's smart. *Too smart.*

Growling, I watch helplessly as he backs her up against a door, his fingers latching onto a loose strand of her hair. You can see her panic in the way she winces away from him and tenses as he lifts the lock toward his face to smell it.

I want to leap through the footage and strangle the fucker. My grip tightens around the phone as Brielle moves on the screen. She's grasping at something behind her, and it isn't until she falls through the doorway of the room that I realize she'd been twisting the knob. *It wasn't locked?*

"He wanted her to find Lincoln's body," I say with certainty.

I may not understand this fucker and his motivations, but that much is clear. Why else would he scare her into this room?

"I want this piece of shit found! Pass out his photo. Search the levels. He has to be here somewhere." My voice is deep, pitched low by the fury building within me.

I don't think I've ever possessed so much *anger*. Even when I lost myself overseas, it doesn't compare to the guilt and fear-fueled rage that boils through me now. I fell asleep. I let my guard down and this asshole got close enough to Brielle to touch her.

Never again.

Joe doesn't hesitate to follow my orders and disappears to direct the rest of his team. While Rhys and I cover the third and fourth floors, the other men will be left to handle the first two, with strict instructions that I be contacted with any findings.

Rhys and I work diligently to scour each mask and check every man left on our levels. There is no video footage of the jackass leaving—in fact, there's *no* security feed after the incident, a bigger issue for another time—so we take our time to ensure we've inspected every inch of the two floors.

It's not until we're clearing the stalls of a restroom on the third floor that my phone buzzes with an incoming text. When I read it, I bolt for the stairs.

Second-floor bar.

It doesn't give any further information, but the message is clear enough. They've found something.

"Brass, what is it?" Rhys is hot on my tail. His long legs keep him close behind me as I all but run down the steps. "Did they find him?"

"I fucking hope so," I grit out.

My entire body is vibrating with adrenaline, but I force myself to slow as we near the entrance to the ballroom. If they've found him, I won't allow him to see that I'm on edge. He doesn't deserve the satisfaction.

Taking a long breath, I slip my brass knuckles over my right hand and push into the room.

I'm surprised to find the space cleared out. Everyone, the patrons and workers that had previously taken up residence within these walls, is gone. All that remain are our hired guards and a single, older gentleman who kneels between them. His mask is gone, but you can see the imprint of where one had been tied in his gelled back, salt-and-pepper hair. He's wearing a black suit, and poking out from beneath his shirt collar, a wolf's head can be seen howling toward his jugular.

My rage moves me forward before my mind can form a coherent thought. I grab the man by the lapels of his jacket and yank him up, my spit flying in his face. "Who the fuck *are* you? What are you doing here?"

"B-Brass. You're not the brother I expected." The man chuckles.

He's nervous. Beads of sweat are collecting along his brow, and his eyes dart around the room.

"We found these on him." Joe holds up a small bag with a singular, white pill inside. "The woman he drugged is on her way to the hospital."

A date-rape drug.

Anger blinds me, and before my brain has the chance to process it or what I've done, Rhys is grabbing my shoulder and pulling me back.

"Not here, Brass." His words bring me back, and I blink as I stare down at the bloodied man lying at my feet.

I don't remember striking him, let alone beating him enough to cause visible damage to his face, but his blood covers my hands. My brass knuckles are soaked with it.

I shrug off Rhys' hand and stalk toward Joe. "Did you check him against the security footage? Where's his mask?"

Joe's jaw visibly ticks, his throat constricting as he swallows and holds out his hand. I don't need to see the thin black eye mask to realize that the fucker lying on the ground behind me *isn't* the one we've been hunting. It's written all over Joe's face.

This isn't the man who murdered Lincoln.

This isn't the man after Brielle.

Fuck.

Fuck!

FUCK!

* * * *

Draven

I swirl the flute of bubbling liquid in my hand and inhale the rich scent of citrus as my fingers trace the worn manilla folder before me. The champagne doesn't compare, and neither will the file's contents after tonight. Not after being so close to her, after touching her, *smelling* her.

My Rose.

Even after being ravaged by those men, with her hair damp from sweat, she still smelled as sweet as I'd imagined. And her body, when it'd momentarily pressed against mine, had been so soft. So pliable…

My cock throbs against my slacks, and I sigh as I set down my glass.

"One last time," I remind myself.

When I next touch my dick, she'll be here, with me. I won't have to imagine or remember. She'll be *mine*.

Flipping open the folder, I flick through the photographs Lincoln compiled for me over the years and smile. Most of his handiwork is displayed on the walls around my home, but these…these are for me and my eyes alone.

Unzipping my fly, I free my growing erection and thumb my favorite glossy image. It's of her undressing, her hair and arms tangled above her head in the top she's removing, revealing her heavy, perky breasts to the camera. More than half of my private collection was taken from a distance, but he managed to take this one from just outside her backdoor. This close, you can see the rosy color of her nipples, see the goosebumps that pebble her skin.

I lick my lips and begin working my hand up and down the length of my shaft. With the smell and feeling of her still so fresh, and my vigorous strokes, I quickly bring myself to the edge of an orgasm. My mind wanders, and I picture her bound to my bed, with her arms trapped above her. I imagine it's *her* hands stroking me, pleasuring me, bringing me to the edge of climax as she confesses her love for me.

Pumping faster and faster, I fuck my hand until I reach my release, my hips rocking as my seed spills into my fist and onto my pants. My head drops back onto the headrest behind me, and I sigh, relishing in the aftershock.

"Soon, Rose."

Very soon.

Chapter Three

Rhys

I twist the satin eye mask over and over in my hands, pacing. A million questions crowd my mind, but with the mess in front of me, I can't focus enough to try to piece any answers together.

"I want him transferred to our tower downtown." I close the distance between me and the unnamed Wolf on the floor. "Do we have a man with the woman he drugged?"

"Yes. I'll be sure to keep you both updated on her condition." Joe nods.

I grunt and nudge the man's face to the side, assessing the damage. His nose is broken in multiple places, the bone crooked or crushed inward, and I suspect — with the blood pooling beneath his skin — that his eye socket is fractured, too. With the extent of swelling, blood and bruises, the fucker is almost unrecognizable. *Shame.*

I glance over my shoulder at Joe. "Did he have anything else on him?"

Joe turns to one of his lackeys and the man produces a cellphone, wallet, a set of keys, and a switchblade. My stomach twists at the sight of the knife, and I growl, my teeth clenched.

This is bad.

Not only were three snakes able to slither into our club, undetected, but they were able to do so with drugs and weapons. There's been a breach in our security, that much is clear, a weak link that put Brielle and our patrons in danger. *We can't let it happen again.*

"Give me that." I point to the weapon as I stand, my chest tight with a swarm of emotions. Anger and annoyance. Fear and guilt. Shame and embarrassment. We are the *Grimm Brothers,* for fuck's sake. How could this happen? "Find and dispose of his car and the rest of his things. We'll touch base with Beast before meeting you downtown."

Tense, I wave the men off and slide my eyes to where Everett is brooding. He's wiping his blood-stained knuckles on his jeans as I approach, his lips pressed into a firm slant.

"I'll call Xander," he mutters when I reach him, forgoing his attempt to clean his hands.

He reaches into his pocket and pulls out his cell, his thumb quick to move across the screen.

"No. We'll go home and debrief him there. We've got time and you"—I snatch the phone from his hands—"need to see our girl."

I'm not above beating a bad man to a bloody pulp— hell, I've done it too many times to count—but he lost himself to his rage tonight. I won't pretend I didn't notice it, notice him slipping back toward becoming the man of his past. The lost soul he'd been before Xander helped him create this club. His safe place to explore healthy alternatives to express his rage. Xander may not have been able to do something like that to help himself, but he's always done whatever it takes to keep us safe. Part of me wonders if, subconsciously, that's why he took Brielle. He knew we needed something he couldn't provide, something to keep us all glued together. She's been our missing piece since she arrived, and I know she can ground Everett in a way Xander and I never could. She'll keep him from losing himself again.

I'm prepared for Everett to argue with me. To insist that I'm wasting time we could be using getting closer to the man threatening Brielle, and our lives together. I'm so certain that I begin readying a rebuttal, but instead of the disagreement I'd been anticipating, he simply nods.

"Okay."

* * * *

I'm not surprised to see that, despite the late hour, Brielle is still awake when we get home. She nearly jumps off the couch when we come through the door, her eyes widening in a momentary lapse of fear before Xander secures her against his side.

"Did you find the fucker?"

I can hear the anger in his voice, *see* it in his tense shoulders and hardened jaw as he waits for a response. I know from reading him that he's close to exploding, and yet the arm banded around Brielle's waist remains gentle. He's being careful with her, protecting her from pain, subconsciously. How can I swoop in and destroy whatever hope she has left?

"No." The small declaration of defeat washes the remaining color from her pale features.

"He's...still out there?" she whispers.

"We'll find him, pet." Everett crosses the room and lowers himself onto the coffee table in front of her.

He strokes her knee, the movement showcasing the blood dried to his knuckles and she gasps.

"Are you hurt?" She grabs his hand to inspect it, but he tugs it back and shakes his head.

"I'm fine. This is another issue my brothers and I will have to deal with."

Xander tenses, his ice-blue gaze sliding to me as I come to sit on the opposite side of Brielle. "What issue?"

"Another Wolf got in tonight and spiked a woman's drink," I explain.

Xander growls and Brielle shivers beside me, her teeth sinking into her lower lip.

"Is she okay?" she shifts, as if attempting to prepare herself for my answer.

I nod and grab her hand, my thumb moving in slow, soothing circles across its back. "Yes. Our men intervened before anything happened and she was taken to a hospital."

"Where is *he*?" Xander questions through his teeth.

"Downtown," Everett replies, grabbing his phone and scanning the screen. "Joe will let us know when he's conscious."

"We should head there now. I don't want to waste any more fucking time," Xander curses.

He stands, and Brielle blanches, her hand groping the empty air after him as she begins drowning at the sudden loss of his body against hers.

"Wait!" She panics and clutches my hand, stilling me as I begin to rise. "What if something happens? You can't go."

"Brielle, you're safe here—"

"I'm not worried about me," she interrupts. Her hand trembles in mine and she grabs onto the leg of Everett's jeans, determined to keep us rooted beside her. "This is getting out of hand and I can't...I can't lose you three, too."

My heart drops at her words. She's already lost *so* much. Her home. Her family. Her freedom. How can we threaten to take what little she does have left?

Xander crosses back toward us and strokes a hand through her waves. He looks between Everett and me, seemingly as lost as I feel. How do we help? How do we keep her grounded in this storm?

"I'll stay here with you, pet," Everett offers. He reaches forward and pries her lower lip free of her teeth, frowning at the blood that's begun to discolor her pink flesh. "Rhys can send us updates to let us know they're safe."

She looks between the three of us and frowns. "You have to go?"

"We need to see what this Wolf knows, Amour," Xander confirms gently.

"You'll let us know you're safe?" She looks to me now.

"I promise, Flower."

Chapter Four

Brielle

"Do you need a distraction, pet?"

The heat of Everett's voice caresses the shell of my ear, grounding me and dragging me out of my thoughts.

Rhys and Xander just disappeared through the garage door, and my chest feels tight with their absence. Too tight. In the years following my mother's death, my anxiety has never been this intense, this heavy. I can't breathe without them here, and knowing my unnamed threat is out there only makes it worse.

"Yes, sir." I nod.

I'm not sure what sort of *distraction* I'm agreeing to, but anything is better than the dark place my mind has fallen into. Anything. Especially, if that *anything* includes, him, me, and a bed.

Hesitantly, I pull my gaze up and flick it over his face. He'd been angry when he'd arrived back home and although it still lingers behind his eyes, the tension in his shoulders has evaporated with my agreement.

He holds out his hand. "Come on. I've got an idea."

I take it and follow him as he stands and starts for the stairs.

"What's your idea?" I ask.

He glances at me over his shoulder as he tugs me down the hall toward his bedroom.

"Do you trust me?" He opens his door, pulls me past the threshold, and seals it shut behind us.

"Of course I do." My reply is instant.

I trust him. I trust all of them with every fiber of my being—body, mind and soul.

He smiles a warm, happy grin, and runs a hand down my back, unzipping my dress with the movement.

He nods toward the floor. "Kneel."

I step out of my dress and drop to my knees, my brow quirked at him in curiosity.

"Close your eyes," he orders, tucking a finger beneath my chin. He stoops down as my eyes close, and presses a gentle, fleeting kiss against my lips. "Don't move."

I can hear his footsteps as they retreat across the carpet, and I frown as I struggle to resist opening my eyes. *Where is he going? What is he doing?*

"Remind me of your safe words." His voice comes from across the room, and I turn my face toward it.

"Yellow and red."

Confirming the two colors sends an excited shiver down my spine, and I relax a little, comforted by the reminder that *I'm* in control in this house, under this roof.

"Good girl."

He's back in front of me, his praise raining down from above, and I jump as something soft brushes my cheek.

"Do you remember our first night at Once Upon a Time, pet?" His low growl makes my thighs press together with need.

"Yes, sir," I reply, my body writhing as he drags the unknown object down my neck and across my exposed shoulder.

"What do you remember?" he asks.

"You...fingering me under the table." My words catch as he uses the mysterious tool to trace around my nipple. "Our waitress, and the nipple clamps."

"What else?"

I want to open my eyes. I want to see what it is that he's teasing me with. I want to watch as it drags down the gully of my breasts, to the slope of my stomach where it hovers just above my pubic bone. That's when I realize what he's holding.

"The riding crop."

A sharp snap sounds through the room, and a warm sting blossoms across my thigh. I squeal, about to open my eyes when his hand grabs my chin, and his breath fans across my face.

"Keep them closed, pet."

Pulling in a steady breath, I can't help but squirm as he slides the crop back up my body to rest beneath my chin. He uses it to guide my head back, and then, it snaps lightly across my breast. The sting of it striking me travels straight to my core, and I moan, rocking my hips.

"You like this, hm?" His deep, raspy voice reverberates through my body, sending a wave of goosebumps over my skin.

I breathe out, shaky with adrenaline and need. "Yes."

He uses the crop to deliver another, harder, snap to my thigh and I gasp as the leather bites into my skin. *Fuck.*

"Open your legs for me, pet. I want to see that wet pussy," he demands.

I move, opening my legs in compliance. Completely bare, I can feel the cool air of the room as it licks against my center, and the rush of wind before another snap bites into my opposite thigh.

"Wider."

I can almost hear the smirk that curls onto his lips.

I spread myself, stretching my legs until I'm knelt with them shoulder-width apart. He groans his approval and lightly trails the leather tongue up my inner thigh. I gasp when it touches my clit, the jolt of electricity coiling deep in my stomach.

"Please, sir." I bite my lip and tilt my pelvis forward enough that I'm granted one glorious second of friction. "Please."

"Needy little thing," Everett muses.

He pulls the crop back before I can press myself against it again, and I whine until the snap of it between my legs silences me.

"Oh, god." My head drops back, and he chuckles, lightly striking me again.

The burning warmth of pain melts into pleasure as the leather snaps against my clit, and I jolt, already close to coming apart.

"Open your eyes, pet," he commands. I peel my eyes open to find him holding the crop close to my face, his hooded gaze alight with flames. "Look at the wet mess you left on my crop. Dirty girl."

My gaze flicks over the strip of leather, and sure enough, it's wet with my arousal. An unexpected giggle escapes me and, feeling bold, I dart my tongue out for a taste. A mixture of flavors explodes across my tastebuds—earthy and smoky from the leather, and sweet and soapy from me. It's intriguing, and so inexplicably *sexy*.

"Pet." Everett's low murmur snags my attention.

His fist has tightened around the crop and his jaw ticks with the effort to keep himself under control.

"Yes, sir?" I ask sweetly.

His cock visibly jumps at my words and he crooks his finger. "Up."

I stand, my legs a little unsteady from the edge I'd been tiptoeing, and gasp when his calloused hand clasps my ass. He hauls me against him and crashes his lips to mine in a searing kiss.

I melt into him, my body molding to his as he drops the crop and cages me in with his large arms. He squeezes my ass, a playful grope as he licks the seam of my mouth, searching for acceptance. When I open for him, he groans, and his tongue slides greedily into my mouth, exploring me, *claiming* me.

My pussy pulses between my legs, and I whimper as my need skyrockets with each tender stroke of his tongue.

"Everett."

He understands the demand in my tone, and slides a leg forward between mine, pressing his thigh into me without breaking the kiss. I groan and rub myself against the denim, taking my pleasure from him.

"That's right, pet. Make yourself feel good," he growls.

It only takes a few hurried thrusts to come apart, my orgasm rippling through me on a broken cry. After everything that's happened tonight, my body goes weak enough that I'd fall if not for his thigh holding me steady.

He breaks the kiss and lifts me into his arms, grinning. "My turn."

He carries me back toward his bed and sets me on my feet, turning me so that I'm facing away from him. I'm confused at first—why didn't he lay me *on* it?—until his hand runs up my spine, guiding me down so my chest hits the sheets. He smacks my ass and captures my left wrist between his fingers, his grip firm but not tight as he guides it behind me. Pinning it in place, I feel the head of his cock as he lines himself up at my entrance.

"Ready, pet?"

I nod and bite my lip, heat creeping up my neck as anticipation swells in my gut. He chuckles and pushes himself in, slow and steady. It burns for a second, a reminder of our fun earlier this evening, before melting into the pleasure I've grown to crave.

"God, Everett." I groan as he fills me, my hips pressing back to meet him.

"Hang on, pet." He grunts.

His hand tightens around my wrist and the other fists my hair, tugging my head back so I'm arched beneath him. He pulls out, his pace just as measured as when he'd entered me, and slides back in. Faster. *Please, faster.* He laughs darkly as he slides back out, and as if reading my thoughts, slams back into me.

"Brass!" I cry out.

He's rocking into me, his rhythm rough and disjointed. My stomach coils, my pleasure skyrocketing as my sensitive pussy clamps around him. He groans and pumps into me hard enough that my feet come off the floor, leaving me a writhing, moaning mess beneath him.

"Yes, yes, yes!" I scream as the edge claws closer.

His thrusts are erratic now as his climax nears, and I bounce back against him until we're both falling over the cliff.

He finishes over my back, and we fall onto the bed together, a panting pile of loose limbs and erratic heartbeats. I curl into his side, my hand sliding up his chest.

"Sleep, pet. I'll wake you if there's news." He kisses my forehead as my eyes slip closed.

I drift off without another thought.

Chapter Five

Xander

I drag my fingertip across the knife's serrated edge, testing the sharpness. Little beads of blood swell and collect along the line where the blade cuts me, and I growl, my eyes sliding to the man in front of me.

"I didn't know he was going to be there, I swear."

Timothy Warsaw, the fucker who smuggled a weapon—a hunting-grade switchblade no fucking less—and drugs into my club, is shaking his head back and forth. He's barely lucid, his injuries more extensive than I'd anticipated, but he still manages to tug at his restraints.

Good.

This wouldn't be any fun for me if the fucker didn't have any fight left in him.

"So, it was all a coincidence then, hm?" I muse, glancing over my shoulder toward Rhys. He's sitting on one of the barstools behind me, his ignited lighter flipping over his fingers as he toys with it. His angry gaze doesn't leave the man in front of me, despite the audible *szzz* as the fire singes his skin, making him appear more intimidating. I smirk. "What do you think, Blaze?"

"The room was in his name. That doesn't sound like a fucking *coincidence* to me," he growls.

"Room? What room? I-I don't know—"

"The room Lincoln was murdered in. It was rented out under your name, Tim." I shorten his name as I step toward him, a low chuckle leaving me as the fucker winces back against the wall.

We'd gotten an update from Joe on the drive here and, while the woman who was drugged will make a full recovery, the information we've been provided with has ensured the piece of shit hanging in front of me *won't*. The room Lincoln died in was rented out in Timothy's fucking name. It was paid for in *cash* and while some form of card—credit, or debit—is normally held in that circumstance to protect against damages and theft, his was never collected. It was still in his fucking *wallet* when Joe confiscated his belongings at the bar, which leaves us with a few different problems.

Our first problem is that this *fuck* had enough money on his person to pay for one of our private rooms in the first place. The premium rooms come with a premium price, which normally secures them far out of affordability for lowlifes, like Tim. So where did he get the money? His bank accounts are close to overdrafting. He *shouldn't* have had access to that amount of cash. But he did. He had enough for the room and enough to pay one of our staff off so they wouldn't keep his card on file. That brings us to our second issue. One of our staff took the bribe. If *that* weren't problematic enough, now we have to figure out who and *why*. Why would they take a bribe from a Wolf? Why weren't they afraid of the repercussions doing so would bring? Why weren't they afraid of the Grimm Brothers? Are they another member of the Wolves?

The thought makes me see red.

I want fucking answers!

"I-I don't understand. This doesn't make any sense," Tim whines. "I wasn't there to cause any trouble."

"Well, we all know *that's* bullshit." Rhys flicks his thumb over the spark wheel of the lighter, sending a soft *stsk* echoing through the room.

"I didn't mean to cause trouble with *you*," he corrects, his head dropping forward in surrender. "I just wanted a good time. It's not easy for a guy like me to get a pretty thing to go home with him. Not all women put out. Like *yours*."

He spits the insult in a fatal attempt to appear tough, as if his body isn't already contorting in fear. As if his *toughness* will earn him anything other than more pain. He's going to learn. I'll show him what insulting my woman *earns* him.

I take the step to close the remaining distance between us and ignore his squirming attempts to get away from me. Grabbing him by the ear, I smirk down at him as panic fills his eyes, and cut. The blade in my hand slices through his cartilage with little to no effort on my end, and blood pours from the fresh opening as his ear comes off in my hand. He screams, his entire body contorting as he fights the restraints holding him fast against the wall.

"Fuck! What the fuck?" He's cursing, his eyes wide with disbelief, pain, fear and disgust as I drop the decapitated appendage to the floor. "Goddammit! You fucking...fuc..."

His head slumps back against the wall, and as his voice trails off, his eyes roll shut. I grit my teeth in annoyance as he faints, and barely resist the urge to plunge the blade of my weapon into his windpipe for good measure.

He isn't allowed to die yet.

"Blaze." I wave my brother forward and pass him the knife. With a nod in the unconscious man's direction, I mutter, "Cauterize it. This fucker isn't getting out of this that easy."

He smirks and holds up his lighter. Igniting it, he drags the flame along the length of the blade, heating the metal. Once the silver-colored steel changes from tan to brown, brown to purple, and finally, purple to blue, he stalks toward Tim. Snarling, he presses the hot metal against the bloody opening on the side of the man's head. The smell of burning flesh rises with the sound of blood popping and sizzling against the heated weapon. It's a symphony of torture, and the pain brings Timothy back.

He screams as he comes to, and continues long after Rhys has pulled the blade away from his skull. When his voice turns raw and he looks like he's about to pass out again—his face drained of its remaining color—I lose what little patience I had left.

"Shut the fuck up!" I bark.

I slam my fist into his stomach, and when he hunches over, finally silenced, I grab him by the hair. With a forceful yank, I lock his head back and hold my hand out for the knife. Rhys passes it to me, and with the threateningly hot metal in my grasp, I lean in close to Tim.

"Scream again, and I'll start pulling out your fucking teeth," I threaten, and when he whimpers, I press the flat edge of the blade against his cheek, burning him. "Maybe you'd prefer I take the other ear?"

His lips tremble with the effort of keeping another round of shouts subdued, the effort audible in the throaty whimpers that do slip from him. At his compliance, I pull the knife away from his face and grin as a piece of his flesh peels off with it.

"I-I'll st...stop," he confirms with a shudder, his forehead dripping with sweat.

I step back, enough to allow Rhys a position in front of Tim and nod my approval for him to take over. If I want to change, for them and Brielle, I have to learn to let go of the reins. *I will be better for her.*

"That's really good, Tim, because we sure as *fuck* didn't bring you here to listen to that shit. We want our answers. Now." Rhys steps forward a fraction of a step, and Tim winces in his bindings.

"W-what answers?" Tim chokes the question out around another whimper.

"Where did you get the money to rent out the room? Who ordered you to kill Lincoln?" Rhys questions.

"I didn't do it." Tim has managed to catch his breath, but his shoulders still heave with the effort to remain calm. "I didn't rent any room, and I didn't kill Lincoln. I didn't even know he was there, I swear to God."

His eyes drop to the floor where his ear lies and he gags. He manages to swallow back his disgust and squeezes his eyes shut before continuing.

"He told me about the masquerade night, but I had no idea he'd be idiotic enough to go. Everyone in the gang knew you three were looking for him." He pauses and swallows again. "No one's seen him around for a while, so I was surprised when he called —"

"Get to the fucking point!" Rhys snaps.

"I-I was just there to get some ass. I thought I'd have an easier time with the masks, and if I didn't, I had the pills as a backup..." He must sense our growing anger because he quickly stops and steers the conversation back to what we *want* to hear. "I don't have any money, but Lincoln does. *Did.* He was always bragging about the cash hookup he had. He must have paid for the room, and put it under my name or something."

He pries his eyes open in an attempt to assess our reactions as we ponder the information he's provided. Lincoln shouldn't have had access to the amount of cash Tim is alluding to. Even running a few jobs for the Wolves here and there wouldn't be enough to...

"Where was the money coming from?" Rhys presses, attempting to piece together the incomplete puzzle Tim is painting for us.

None of this makes sense.

"He got it doing odd jobs from some guy he called D."

D. It's not a name, but it's *something*. Who knew all it took to get this little piggy to squeal was taking an ear?

"*Like...?*"

You can hear the irritation growing in Rhys' normally collected voice. This fucker may be giving us information, but he's doing it in broken, incomplete segments. It's infuriating.

I want to snap his fucking neck.

"Photography, mostly. It sounded like D wanted pictures of Rose. *Only* Rose. The better the photo, the better he'd pay," Tim pants out the explanation and drops his head back against the wall, exhausted. He takes a few sputtering breaths, and I grind my teeth at the pause in his story before he continues. "D wanted them every day, so i-if Lincoln couldn't provide them for some reason, he'd have whatever fuck he could con into doing it for the lowest cut take the pictures for him. You know the type. Guys like…like — "

"Like Scout Madden," I finish for him, my hands balling into tight fists at my sides. That's why Brielle recognized him in the basement. "They were stalking her."

"I-I guess you could call it that." Tim chuckles nervously, his eyes shifting between Rhys and me.

I try not to let the thought provoke me, or threaten the anger I'm barely keeping a handle on, but it does. They've been following her, taking pictures of her, for *years.*

Why?

"And you know all of this from a few drunken conversations with Lincoln?" Rhys doesn't hide the disbelief lurking in his voice as he steps closer to Tim. "It sounds like you were pretty involved with the situation, yourself."

"I wasn't. I wasn't. L-Lincoln just talked a lot." *That's probably what got him killed.* "But that's all I know, I swear."

Rhys looks to me for guidance now, and I smirk as I reclaim Timothy's attention.

"You've been a good little wolf today, Tim. It's a shame you planned to rape someone at my club. If not for that, who knows? Maybe I would have let you live."

Chapter Six

Brielle

Voices stir me awake.

I sit up, feeling groggy from the lack of sleep—*and orgasms*—and strain my ears, listening. Xander's low tenor carries into Everett's room, and although he's too far away for me to make out what he's saying, I still scramble out of bed. *They're home.* Did they find anything? Did they find *him?*

My mind fills with images of the masked man from the hall, and in my distraction, I don't notice Rhys has slipped into the room until I run into him.

Literally.

He chuckles, the light sound of his laugh melting my fears as his arms encircle my waist to keep me from stumbling backward.

"Well, hello, Flower." His lips press against my forehead, and I bury my face into his chest, inhaling his scent.

His normal spicy aroma is masked by something else, something burnt, so I pull back enough to do a quick scan for injuries. When I don't find any burns, I release a sigh of relief and lean back into him.

"You're home," I murmur.

"I am now that I'm holding you." His words make my heart flutter and my belly flip, like I'm some little girl with a schoolyard crush. "What're you doing awake?"

I frown, hating the fear that quickly evaporates the nonsensical joy that had filled my chest. *Did they find him?*

"I heard Xander. I wasn't sure if... Did you—" I pause and try to steady my voice. "Did you find anything?"

His lips twist, as if he's contemplating his answer. "We got a few answers, yes."

His gentle response isn't what I expect to hear. It stalls the air in my lungs and my heart palpitates with anxiety as my mind runs rampant with questions. Despite being hopeful that this mess was drawing nearer to its end, I never anticipated actually making the needed progress. My mouth opens and closes, unable to form any of the words booming through my skull.

"Why don't you get dressed and we'll go downstairs to get you something to eat? We can talk while I cook." His fingers skim my back, and I flush, only now remembering that I'm still bare from my time with Everett.

"I'll throw on a tee, but I don't think I'll be able to—"

"Breakfast wasn't a suggestion, Flower. You need to eat." His voice is stern as he interrupts me, and despite the smile that pulls onto my lips, I roll my eyes.

"You sound like your brother," I tease.

"Yeah? Should I bend you over my knee for rolling your eyes at me, then?"

He slaps my ass and I giggle, playfully pushing at his chest in an attempt to wriggle away. Just like that, he's able to put my mind at ease again.

"Fine, fine! I'll try to eat, but I want answers first."

"Promise?"

"I promise."

We're finally getting closer to ending this hell that's destroyed my family... *Right?*

* * * *

By the time Rhys is finished cooking my mandatory breakfast, I'm shaking. My men are speaking, their voices low and steady as they attempt to formulate a plan, but their words don't register. I'm too distraught to hear them.

He's gone.

The masked man, my elusive stalker, has disappeared into the shadows, and with him went any security footage that may have been used to identify him. Outside shots of the parking lot, that would have captured his car and a traceable license plate. Video feed from the first floor, where he would have provided a photo I.D. to register. It's all gone. Deleted. *Destroyed.*

He's proving to be smart, wealthy, powerful—a deadly combination that allows him to always stays one step ahead of us. We were wrong to think we could lure him into a trap. We were wrong to think that I'd ever be safe from him. *He's untouchable.*

D.

That's all we know about him — an *initial*. My unnamed threat, who wields money like a weapon, provided that pseudonym for the men he employed to photograph me. To stalk me. *D*. One. Single. Letter.

I try to conjure a memory, a face, or something that could point us toward discovering his true identity, but nothing comes to mind. He's been having me followed for god knows how long, and I can't even imagine what his fucking name could be. *Who is he?* Why *me*? He could have anyone, *anything*, yet, he's after me. He wants *me*.

Why?

A hand touches mine and I jump, falling out of my thoughts.

"Flower, please eat something."

I blink at the untouched plate of food in front of me and frown.

"You promised you'd try."

The reminder settles like a heavy weight in my stomach, making me sigh as I pick up my fork.

"Just a few bites, pet," Everett murmurs beside me.

I sigh and scoop up a forkful of egg. I scan my men as I lift the bite to my lips, and do my best to ignore the sour taste the food leaves in my mouth. Rhys is standing across the island from me, his green eyes scouring my face as if doing so will allow him to read my mind. He looks worried, and as I glance between the other brothers, I realize he isn't the only one. Everett, who is sitting in the chair next to me, has his eyebrows furrowed as he studies me. Xander is hovering beside me, his hand on top of mine, his thumb stroking a small path along the top of my knuckles.

"I-is there a way to see my father? Maybe he knows—" My men share a look amongst themselves, and a lump forms in my throat. *Something happened.* Something they don't want to share with me. "What? What is it?"

"Your father is on a psychiatric hold, Amour. No one can see him while he's in solitary. *We* can't even get access to him right now." Xander is trying to tiptoe around the situation as if doing so will keep my world from falling apart.

It doesn't.

I spiral, trying to grasp what's happening. They've isolated him. Locked him in a room, alone. *Why?* Did D do this? Is it another form of punishment? Another way to torture my family?

"Flower." Rhys pulls me out of my wandering thoughts. "He's going through withdrawal. He isn't himself right now—"

"They think he's dangerous?" I mutter, unable to wrap my mind around the idea. It's laughable. My father isn't...

"He attacked another inmate, pet." Everett's words knock the air out of my lungs. I gape and pull in a rough, short breath. "He tried to hurt himself, too."

I wince as guilt and anger swarm me, weighing down my already heavy heart. "This is my fault."

"No, Flower," Rhys argues, but I shake my head and push away from the island.

"My father's in prison. He's detoxing from drugs that were forced into his system, and Sammy is missing. God only knows where he is, and you three—" I stop as I look between my men, my eyes burning with unshed tears. "I've caused so much trouble for all of you."

"Amour, stop this." Xander closes the small distance between us and grabs my face, his rough palms cupping my cheeks. "Don't let him into your head. Don't let him win."

Tears spill down my face, and he swipes them away with the gentle caress of his thumb.

"We're all in this together, Brielle. We're in each other's lives. You're ours. It's too late to go back now."

Theirs.

I lean into Xander's caress and glance at the other two brothers. They've moved closer, and as I reach for them, they encircle me, holding me gently between them.

"He will *not* win," I confirm.

If only speaking the words were enough to end this mess…

Chapter Seven

Everett

Over the next few days, Brielle floats somewhere between the roles of distraught daughter and determined retaliator. I can see her trying to hide her pain and the hurt of having her family torn apart, but there's no disguising the anger in her gaze — the heat of a flame stoked by the need for revenge. Not from us, anyway. Not from three men who've grown accustomed to seeing that glow burning in their own reflections.

I scan her now, inspecting her sleeping form. She's curled up on the couch, a tablet with looping security footage flashing a blue shadow across her face. The color darkens the appearance of the circles beneath her eyes, and I frown, knowing she's lost more than a few hours of sleep to the damn screen in her hands. She's been inspecting every frame of available video over and over in the feeble hope of spotting a familiar face among the crowds. We've warned her more than once that it's a futile mission, but our woman is nothing if not insistent. She wants to feel useful — her words — so if scouring the same reel numerous times is what she needs to achieve that feeling, then dammit, who are we to deny her?

I cross the room and gently lift the tablet from her loose grip. She stirs slightly, and a low whine escapes her parted lips at the loss of the device, but she doesn't wake.

Thank fuck. She needs the rest.

I set it down on the coffee table and contemplate moving her upstairs. I know she'd be more comfortable in a bed, but if she wakes in the transfer, I doubt she'd go back to sleep.

"You're going to be late." Rhys' sudden intrusion cuts into my wandering thoughts, and I scowl, motioning for him to be quiet.

If he wakes her up, I swear to god...

I grab the blanket off the back of the couch, drape it over Brielle, and retreat with a sigh. Once I reach Rhys, I pause for a beat, and we watch her together in silence. She looks so peaceful, lying there. More peaceful than she has in days. At least the monsters that come alive while she dreams seem to be leaving her alone, for now.

She shifts, a hand lifting to scratch her cheek, and like a magnet, Rhys is pulled a step closer. My eyes drift from our sleeping woman and I watch with a mixture of surprise and fear as my brother's face changes, his gaze melting from one of concern to...something else. Something far more dangerous.

Love.

I'm not sure if he realizes what's happened, if he can sense the change that's just happened, or if he's blind to it, but *I* see it. I see it and I understand that, despite whatever happens, everything is different now. Up until this point, there'd been a chance she'd walk away after this. There'd been a chance that we'd *let* her if that's what she chose to do, but that won't happen now. We won't allow it. She's going to be stuck with us until there's no more air left in our goddamn lungs.

"What are you two doing?" We both freeze and turn, wide-eyed, toward the scolding, maternal voice that's come from behind us. Mrs. Claebourne is hovering just inside the open front door, a caddy of cleaning supplies nestled in the crook of her arm. She's watching us with pursed lips and narrowed eyes, her wrinkled finger shaking at us disapprovingly. "You leave that poor girl be, she must be exhausted."

"I'm so glad that you didn't forget while away on vacation that *we're* the ones who dish out the orders around here," I tease with a smile.

It's been a few weeks since we last saw the old woman. Xander insisted she take some time off after the attack and covered every expense to ensure she wouldn't have a reason to decline. Her absence has been noticeable, and not just in terms of housekeeping. Her presence alone is enough to warm the space in a way only a motherly figure can.

"Well, *I'm* glad to see that you three can manage to keep a house semi-tidy in my absence," she shoots back with a wink.

I pull her into a hug, attempting and failing to hold in a bout of light laughter. If she's pleased that the front rooms are tidy, she'll be ecstatic when she sees Brielle's. I don't have the balls to explain to her that the room is so pristine because it's rarely used. Our woman prefers to sleep with us.

"Go on, now. Scat. You've got somewhere to be, don't you?" She pats my chest and raises a brow at Rhys. "If you've got nothing else to do, I'm sure I can find something for you to clean. Lord knows there are plenty of bathrooms in this house."

She pulls a duster free from her caddy and shakes it between us, a mischievous grin lighting up her face. I hold up my hands, and back toward the garage, cackling as she whacks Rhys over the head with it.

"All right, all right I'm leaving." I shoot a look at Rhys, who's failing to block off her light blows. "Tell Brielle I'll be back later tonight, and try to get her to eat something."

"Yes, sir." Rhys tosses a mock salute in my direction and yelps as another swat lands along the back of his head.

Mrs. Claebourne slides her eyes to me, her brow raised in silent question as she waggles the duster in my direction. I take the opportunity to flee, laughing as Rhys continues to throw out whispered cries and pleas for mercy.

He'd better not wake her.

The thought follows me, repeating over and over in my mind as I slide behind the wheel of my car and maneuver it down the driveway. She's not slept well or eaten a full meal since the incident at the club, and I can only hope that she'll do better today. If we're lucky, Mrs. Claebourne will bake something for her to eat. If the old woman finds out how long it's been since she's cleared her plate, she'll be serving our heads for dinner.

I merge onto the highway, heading in the direction of the city so I can check on our tower downtown. We had a crew in to cleanup after our most recent interrogation, and while we don't mind a little mess left behind, I've got to make sure the body's gone. We don't want to hold onto a Wolf longer than we have to.

My phone pings and a text comes over the speakers in the generic, robotic smartphone voice. It's Xander, letting us know that that he's on his way back to the house after doing his rounds. He wants an update on Brielle, but before I can press the button to call him, another text pings through the car. This time, it's Rhys, confirming that she's asleep on the couch, and a small weight seems to lift off my shoulders at the notification.

She's sleeping.

She's *still* sleeping.

Today is going to be better, it has to be.

We're going to make her whole again, one way or another.

Chapter Eight

Brielle

The feeling of strong arms encircling me filters through the sleep clouding my brain, and for a moment, I'm weightless as they lift me. Still exhausted, I melt into their hold and move my lips in a soundless complaint.

I was comfy.

"I've got you, Flower." Rhys' gentle voice fans across my face, and I sigh, nuzzling into his chest. *I suppose this is better.* "Go back to sleep."

The gentle sway of his stride as he carries me through the house lulls me back to the peaceful brink of sleep. I have an underlying urge to fight it, but the unrelenting desperation to continue pushing for answers feels distant. It's more distant than it's been in days.

Sleep.

Sleep...

My mind chants the order, over and over again until Rhys lays me in his bed. Everything goes quiet once I'm there, wrapped in his arms and scent. I breathe out a quiet moan, and Rhys chuckles, pulling me closer to him. *I love you.* The thought, the *realization*, whispers across my otherwise silent mind, and a smile flitters across my lips as I drift.

I love him.

I am in love with one of the Grimm Brothers.

* * * *

Draven

"Everything you asked for is in here." The man retrieves a duffle bag from the trunk of his car and turns back to me. "I can show you how to assemble it if —"

"That won't be necessary," I interrupt.

The less time I spend here, the better.

I hold out my hand, but he hesitates, his eyes flicking over the hood and sunglasses concealing my face. "Are you sure? Suppressors can be kind of intimidating if you've never used one."

I drop my chin and retrieve a thick stack of cash from my pocket. "I'm sure."

Just take the money and go.

I hold out the wad and at the flash of green, the man moves to finish the exchange. With the bag in my hand, I nod my thanks and turn with a grin back toward my vehicle, feeling empowered.

There will be no escaping me, now.

"Wait, you gave me too much," the man calls, but I wave him off with a growl.

"Keep it."

For a man selling a gun—complete with a silencer, clips, and ammo—off the internet to a stranger, he seems far more straight-laced than I'd anticipated. I roll my eyes and slip into the car before he can say anything else, slamming the door shut behind me. Dropping the duffel onto the passenger seat, I open it and glance down at the black weapon lying amongst the cases of bullets.

I'm one step closer, Rose.

Now, to bring you home.

* * * *

Brielle

I love you, too.

The words echo through my ears as I wake, far off enough to seem like a forgotten dream, but close enough to have me questioning their validity. *Did I imagine it?* Or did he, did *we*, really say…?

Crack. Boom!

The sound of thunder crashes overhead, and the arms around me jolt, knocking me out of my clouded thoughts.

"Fuck." The curse falls into the room as loudly as the downpour beginning to pelt the roof, and I pry my eyes open, worried. "Dammit, I'm sorry, Flower. I didn't mean to wake you."

"You didn't." I watch as his green eyes jump from me to the ceiling. "Rhys?" His eyebrows are knit together, creating a deep wrinkle between them, and his entire body is rigid beside me. "Are you okay? What's wrong?"

Panic lances through me and I drag my hands along his chest, impulsively examining him for injuries.

"Everything's fine, Flower. I'm sorry. It's just the storm," he murmurs.

Beneath my palm, his heart is beating erratically, the rushed rhythm noticeable through the muscle dividing us, and his skin is slicked with sweat. He won't meet my gaze, his chest rising and falling in short, unfulfilling breaths.

He's...scared.

"I normally have an easier time ignoring them, but this one—"

Another *boom* rips through the house and his jaw clenches, cutting his words short.

The storm.

I nod and drag the pad of my thumb over the crease between his brows, attempting to smooth it out. "What do you need?"

"I'll be okay, Flower." He sighs and closes his eyes, leaning into my touch, "Thunderstorms just bring back...*unpleasant* memories."

Oh, Rhys. The johns...

My stomach roils, and I bite back the questions that form, knowing better than to probe into his mind while he's being haunted. Now is not the time to ask for an explanation. A distraction, though?

That might work.

"Rhys?" I whisper, sliding my hand to the back of his neck. "Can I kiss you?"

He chuckles and opens his eyes. When those green orbs meet mine, they're no longer darkened by fear, but blazing with heat. *Mischief.*

"I'm yours, Flower."

Chapter Nine

Rhys

Her lips are gentle, *hesitant*, as they press against mine. I can sense her worry, feel the fear that any wrong move might break me apart, but she doesn't understand. Having her here, holding me, touching me, *comforting* me, is what I need.

It's all I ever needed.

I pull her into me, roughly, hungrily, and she gasps, surprised. This isn't what she'd been anticipating, but as my hands skate down her body, exploring her curves, she melts into me, granting me the access I need. What had begun as a slow waltz of lips and tongue turns heated.

I bite into her lower lip, and she mewls, my name tumbling out on a hissed breath. "Rhys!"

The breathy sound of my name coming from her goes straight to my dick, bringing it to life and hardening it against her belly. I can feel her smile, a satisfied grin that only driving my desire higher as she grabs the waist of my sweats.

I chuckle, a low, deep rumble as she tugs at my pants, desperate to remove the piece of fabric keeping us separated. I lift my hips, helping her slide them down, and as soon as I'm free, she grabs the base of my cock. Pumping, she slides her hand up and down my shaft, the quick, smooth motion making me jerk beneath her touch.

"Fuck, Flower," I curse.

Her skin is so fucking *soft*. It glides against me with the perfect amount of resistance, making me grit my teeth as my pleasure skyrockets. I have to keep myself under control if I'm going to use our time alone to its full advantage.

Our *first* time alone.

She squirms, and I glance down, watching in amusement as she tries unsuccessfully to tug off her shorts with one hand.

I lean into her and drag my tongue up the shell of her ear. "Would you like some help, Flower?"

"Yes, please." She shivers.

I hook my thumbs into her bottoms and, in one fluid movement, tug her cotton shorts and underwear off. Fuck me, she's so *wet*.

"Goddammit, Flower," I growl, dropping her soaked panties to the floor. "How am I supposed to take my time with you when you're so responsive to my touch?"

She blushes as she swirls my pre-cum around the head of my cock, slicking it with my own desire. "I could say the same for you."

I smirk and grab her thigh. *She's right.*

Hitching her leg over my hip, I drag my hand down her stomach, making her squirm as she continues pumping my cock. When I finally touch her pussy, my finger slipping through her wet folds, she moans and arches into me.

"So *responsive*," I praise.

"*Oh.*" Her mouth falls open as I push a finger into her, curling it up to stroke her g-spot. "Oh, fuck." Her hand, which is still tight around my dick, has stopped moving as she loses herself to the pleasure I'm delivering. "Fuck, Rhys!"

I lean into her and bite her earlobe as I slide another digit inside her. She gasps, her hips moving to meet my thrusts in a desperate attempt to get my fingers deeper.

"Do you want more, Flower?" I ask, grinning as her head bobs up and down. "Hm?"

"Yes. Yes!" She pants.

I claim her lips, snaking my tongue into her mouth as my thumb brushes over her swollen clit. She jolts, and I swallow her moans, the sound of her pleasure hardening my dick to the point of pain as I drive her higher. Her pussy pulses around my fingers, and I stroke her faster, harder, until she comes apart. Her walls clamp around me, and she cries out as she grinds herself into my hand, riding through the waves of her orgasm.

"Good. Good fucking girl," I commend her, my voice a low growl that comes from deep in my chest.

A smile creeps onto her flushed face, and her hooded eyes drop to the space between us, where her hand is still wrapped around me. Her tongue darts out to wet her swollen lower lip and I know without asking that she wants me in her mouth, but...

I'm being selfish, tonight.

I grab her hips and roll, pulling her on top of me. It's a new position for her, and you can see the uncertainty it causes as she hovers over me, hesitant.

"Is this okay?" I ask, checking in with her.

Yes, my Flower has safe words at her disposal, but the look on her face has me searching for a verbal confirmation.

"Yes, I'm just..." She trails off and captures her lip between her teeth.

Her eyes dart away from mine, and I frown, my hand reaching up to take her chin. I force her gaze back to me, and raise a brow, attempting to read her.

"Flower?" I prod.

"I don't know what I'm doing," she finally admits, and an embarrassed sigh escapes her.

I push myself up with one hand and bend my knees, taking her weight and trapping her between me. Her thighs open as she shifts, allowing my cock to press against her center, and she shivers.

"The only thing you need to know is that your pleasure is *my* pleasure," I murmur, trailing my lips along her jaw. "Ride me. Make yourself come on my cock."

My encouragement is all she needs.

She lowers herself and my dick slowly — *oh so fucking slowly* — sinks into her wet cunt, burying me inside her.

God, fuck.

A moan rushes from her once she's settled atop me, and she rolls her hips, testing the position. The movement makes her pussy clench and somehow, my cock slides deeper.

Fuck!

"Oh, Blaze." She tests the movement again, but this time, while circling, she lifts onto her knees, dragging her wet cunt up my shaft.

"Goddamn, Flower," I curse, and thrust up to meet her, chuckling as her mouth falls open in a silent cry. "That's it, Brielle."

She repeats the motion, over and over, finding a rhythm and picking up speed. Rolling and lifting, thrusting and grinding, my dick slides in and out of her as she moves, filling her until her loud cries begin spilling into the room. I grunt and reach between us, finding her sensitive clit and circling it with the pad of my finger.

"Oh, Rhys, yes! Fuck." She arches her back and slides her hands up to cup her breasts.

She pinches her nipples, tugging at the rosy buds until they harden into tight peaks between her fingers. The sight makes me growl, and I drive into her harder, faster, as my climax begins coiling deep in my stomach.

Fuck, fuck, fuck.

Her pussy quivers around me, and then her own orgasm is there, breaking over us.

"Rhys!" She cries out as her walls clamp around me, and I groan, thrusting into her harder as I'm thrown over the edge. I come, still buried deep inside her, and let her pussy milk me of every last drop. Panting, I drop my forehead to hers, and murmur the sentence I've been afraid of admitting since the day I laid my fucking eyes on her.

"I love you, Flower."

Chapter Ten

Brielle

"I love you, Flower."

The words I'd feared were nothing more than a figment of my imagination fall against my face with the warmth of his exhale, solidifying them and their truth. *He loves me...* The realization makes my heart lurch, and I open my eyes, reeling.

"I love you, too."

My admittance makes his breath catch, and something crosses his face — disbelief, surprise, or maybe even a combination — as he watches me. His fingers trace my hip, but other than that gentle stroke, neither of us moves. The room narrows in around us until nothing remains but our hold on one another, and the distant rumble of thunder.

* * * *

I'm not sure how much time passes, how long we sit like that, bundled in each other's arms, but eventually, a light knock at the door stirs us. Rhys blows out a breath and rolls us, dropping me onto the bed beside him with a smirk.

"Lunch is downstairs, whenever you're ready," a familiar voice, a *woman's* voice, calls through the door.

"Mrs. Claebourne?" I ask, embarrassment flooding my face.

She definitely heard us...

"You didn't think we'd keep her away forever, did you?" He chuckles and stands, grabbing his discarded pants from the floor.

"When did she get back?" My legs tingle with pins and needles, keeping me seated on the bed.

"Late this morning." He slides his sweats up his long legs, and turns back to me quickly, "Oh, shit. Everett wanted me to let you know he'd be back tonight."

Oh.

It feels like forever since I've gotten to spend more than a few fleeting minutes with all three of my men, but how can I complain? They're running themselves ragged for *me*.

"Where's the tablet?" I swing my head, guilt spiking as I quickly scan the room for it.

I'd fallen asleep while re-watching the security footage from that night at the club. *How could I do that?* I'm useless unless I find something...

"You can have it back *after* you eat something." Rhys shakes his head, and when I open my mouth to argue, he holds up his hand. "You've lost weight, Flower. I won't watch you wilt away into nothing."

I tuck my bottom lip between my teeth and nod, knowing better than to argue. If I keep worrying them, they won't let me help at all, and I *have* to do something to catch the fucker ruining my family.

"Why don't you hop in the shower, and I'll grab you something to wear?" He leans across the bed and pecks my cheek.

Before he can straighten, I hook my arms around his neck and cling to him. I'm overwhelmed. I'm exhausted. I'm scared, and confused, and *angry*, but...when I'm with them, I'm just theirs. Nothing else matters.

This needs to end so I can just be *theirs.*

"I love you," I murmur into his neck.

He strokes my hair. "I love you."

I pull back and offer him a small half-smile before glancing at the bathroom behind me. "I should probably go shower..."

"Yeah, you should. You stink." He pulls in an exaggerated breath and gags, laughing.

I roll my eyes, giggling as I stand. Lightning crackles through the windows and thunder shakes the glass, but unlike earlier when the noise had jolted him, Rhys remains unaffected. He turns toward the door, still fake gagging. *Good.* I may not be able to erase the memories of his past, but at least I can help him stay here, in the present, with me.

As if reading my thoughts, he turns before he exits the room, and tosses a sly grin in my direction. "I hope our distractions are as efficient for you as that's been for me."

I gape, flushing as he leaves. *I do enjoy their distractions...* Running my fingers through my tangled waves, I turn toward the en suite as the sticky mixture of our releases begins dripping down my skin. It distracts me for a moment, the sudden swell of excitement that comes with memory of him being inside me, but I tamp it down and force myself to focus.

Shower, food, and then surveillance.

It's time to get back on track.

* * * *

I tie my waves back in a messy bun at the nape of my neck, and step into the hall. It's bright, the storm having passed while I was showering, and the smell of Mrs. Claebourne's cooking wafts through the house. It makes my stomach growl, announcing my arrival as I descend the stairs and turn into the living room.

"Someone's hungry." Mrs. Claebourne turns from the stove with a smile. "Hello again, dear."

"Hi." I flush as I slide into a chair at the island, praying my shower got rid of the smell of sweat and sex that had clung to me. "How're you doing, Mrs. —" I pause as she raises a brow, and quickly correct myself. "Claire?"

She nods her approval, and pushes a full plate toward me. "I'm glad to be back at work. I've never been very good at sitting idly by."

"Yeah, me either," I admit, wincing.

Oh, Sammy…

Images of my brother drift through my mind, memories of him as an infant, toddler, and young child that depended on me, *solely* on me. My father wasn't around after mother died, and while I'd like to believe he was working, I now know the truth I've been desperate to ignore for years.

He's a gambler.

That's where he was, the night that mom died. In a casino somewhere, losing the money he needed to pay off her medical bills. That's why he was desperate to get me through college. With a degree, I could get a dependable job. With money, I could cover his losses.

Oh my god.

Cover his losses...

"Feel better, Flower?" Rhys' sudden intrusion makes me jump, and I whip around in my seat to face him.

"I'm collateral." My mind is racing, piecing together the disjointed puzzle that has been my life since my mother's death.

"What? What're you talking about, Flower?" I can hear the confusion in Rhys' voice, but I don't look at him as I begin pacing.

"I'm *collateral*," I repeat, wringing my hands. "All of this, everything that's happened..."

I can't form a coherent sentence, my mind making connections faster than I can speak.

"Flower, I don't—"

"I knew it was bad, but I didn't realize...dammit, why didn't I see it?" I shake my head, and wave off Rhys' hands as he tries to stall me. I feel sick, physically, mentally, as my heart leaps in my chest. My breathing is labored and my voice is shaky as I continue. "The guys he had stalking me, it was just for insurance."

"Brielle, stop, you're not making any sense," Rhys tries, but his voice feels distant.

My father used me as collateral.

D must have lent my father money, and has decided it's time to collect what he's owed. *Me*. This elaborate fucking mess, my missing brother, the torture my father's endured...

It's D collecting interest.

The room tilts on its axis and I stumble, unable to catch my balance. It's not until then, as my legs turn molten and I begin to fall, that I realize I'm close to fainting. I should crash into the unforgiving tile, but strong arms catch my weight, and ease me to the floor.

"Count, Brielle." It's Xander's deep voice that cuts through the panic, the guilt and the *anger* swarming me.

I can feel him beside me, an anchor amidst the raging storm, and squeeze my eyes shut, trying to count. His large hand hooks around the back of my neck, and with the world still rocking around me, I'm powerless as he forces my head between my knees.

"Count," he repeats.

One.

Two.

Three...

"Out loud," Rhys prompts.

"One. Two. Three..." I pause, and blow out a long, slow, exhale. "Four. Five. Six."

The dizziness fades, enough for the discomfort of the position I'm in to become noticeable, and I shift beneath his hold.

"That's it." Xander's thumb strokes over my clammy skin, but he doesn't release me.

"Seven. Eight. Nine," I continue.

His hand moves, shifting to my shoulder so I remain bent over, and something cold, and wet, takes its place.

A rag.

"Keep breathing, Flower." Rhys lowers himself to my opposite side, and squeezes my knee.

Catching my breath, I finish. "Ten."

It's silent now, and I take a moment to collect my scrambled thoughts. With the world still, and my blood pressure returning to normal, I feel more in control than I'd been.

"That's my girl," Xander murmurs, his hand sliding from my shoulder to my lower back. "Take it slow, Amour."

With their hands still holding me, I sit up hesitantly, my face flushed and wet with tears. "I'm sorry."

"We're here, Flower. It's okay," Rhys rumbles, tucking a wayward piece of hair behind my ear.

He eyes Xander over my head, and I follow his gaze, biting my lip as blue eyes bore into mine.

"Better?" he questions, waiting to continue until I've murmured a meek *'yes'*. "Good. Now, why don't you tell us what's going through that pretty head of yours, Amour?"

Chapter Eleven

Xander

It takes some time for Brielle to unravel the thick web of thoughts that have woven their way through her mind. The betrayal she feels is palpable as she explains her theory, but some color returns to her face as she speaks, easing the concern that had tightened my chest.

"Here dear, drink this." Mrs. Claebourne comes around the island with a glass of water in her hand.

She passes it to Brielle, who takes a hesitant sip before glancing between Rhys and me. "I...I just can't think of any other possible explanation for all of this."

I nod, my jaw tight with anger as I attempt to process what she's told us. Sure, a pissed-off usurer with enough power could do the amount of damage that's been done to her family, but *why*? Why would they want to get *us* involved? Why would they continue hunting her after we, the fucking *Grimm Brothers*, have so openly staked our claim on her?

"The Wolves don't have a loan shark on their payroll," Rhys mutters, before his eyes slide to me. "Not a public one, anyway."

Not a public one.

"Rhys, call Everett. Tell him to come home," I grind the words out through my teeth, and stand.

"Xander...? What is it?" Brielle scrambles to follow me, but I'm too distracted to reply.

The back room of that shithole strip club George was taken from. It's rented out to whoever has the money to pay for it, no questions, no documentation, and no names.

At least, that's what they told us.

Of course, the fuckers would have *lied* if they were trying to keep D hidden from us.

"Beast." The fear that's trickled into Brielle's voice stalls me, and I turn to meet her worried gaze. "What's going on?"

I've wandered into the basement, and she's watching me from the last step, confused. The look on her face is nearly identical to the one that had marred her features the last time she'd come down here, and I growl, haunted by what I've exposed her to.

"Go back upstairs, Amour." I don't want her down here, surrounded by the hate and anger I've bloodied the space with.

"You promised you'd try."

The reminder makes me pull in a steadying breath, and I nod, knowing she's right. The man my father tried turning me into wouldn't give two fucks about promises, but the man I'm becoming, the one being shaped for *her*, is going to continue trying.

No more shutting her out.

"I'm sorry, Amour." It's not the first time I've apologized to her, and with my track record, it won't be the last, either, but it still feels foreign rolling off my tongue. "I just..." I pause, trying and struggling to articulate my concern. "This is where it all began."

I watch her eyes drift around the room, taking in the blood-stained floor and the chains still hanging from the ceiling. I want to know what she's thinking. Is the memory of me locking her down here, terrified, confused, and injured running through her mind? Or is the sound of Scout Madden's neck snapping echoing in her ears?

"The things you've seen. The things I've done—"

"You are *not* getting rid of me that easily, Xander Grimm." She interrupts me and shifts her weight, taking the last step into the space. "Neither of us are the same person we were when this all started. We've changed."

She stretches her hand out, reaching for me as she crosses toward me. I don't flinch when she touches me, when her fingers delicately trace the spot where I'd been stabbed, and she smiles at me triumphantly, her point proven.

I sigh, and lift a hand to cup her cheek. "Amour, do you remember the club your father was taken from?"

"Yes." She nods, her brow raising in question.

"It's possible that the workers there lied while Rhys and Everett were questioning them. If they *did*, they'd know what the room is used for, and *who* uses it," I explain, watching as understanding dawns on her.

"They'd know who *D* is," she murmurs.

"Yes." Her breath catches in her throat as I continue. "Once Everett gets home, we'll sit down and discuss what we're going to do."

"When will he be—"

"He's on his way." Rhys steps off the stairs, and turns to access the armory. "What're you thinking, Beast?"

"Automatics," I reply.

Brielle gapes as the stairs lift, revealing the secret room, and curses, "Holy shit..."

"Did you really expect anything less, Amour? We are the Grimm Brothers, after all." I chuckle.

"What if I'd found this while I was snooping around down here? I could have killed you." She blanches.

"Yeah? Do you know how to use a gun, Flower?" Rhys' laughter spills out of the room.

"Don't you just pull the trigger thingy?" The naivety of her question makes me chuckle as I step toward the opening.

"That's how you *fire* it, yes." I reach in and grab my handgun from the counter, and turn back to face her. "But if I handed this to you, would you be able to use it to defend yourself?"

She steps back as I approach her with the weapon, and already, I know we have some work to do. She can't be afraid of guns if she's going to survive in our world.

"I've never fired one," she admits, her eyes widening as I twist the gun around in my hand.

I hold the grip out to her, but she shakes her head and retreats again, her teeth sinking into her bottom lip.

"Amour." My voice is gentle as I lower my hand, hating the uncertainty that's curled her shoulders. "You need to know how to protect yourself."

"I can! Ask Rhys, I've got my gut punch down solid." She waves her hand toward the armory, exasperated.

"She really does." He leans out of the room and rubs at his stomach with an exaggerated groan.

"You are *not* fucking helping." I glower at him and he shrugs, smirking at me before he ducks away again. Rolling my eyes, I turn my attention back to Brielle. "Come on, Amour. Let me show you how to hold it."

She slides forward a fraction of an inch and puffs out a small breath. "It just makes me nervous. They can cause so much damage."

"The person wielding it controls the amount of damage that is done, Amour. If they're predictable and skilled, the risk to someone other than the target is lower." I reach for her, and skim my fingers over the back of her hand. "Do you trust me, Brielle...?"

Her hazel eyes lift to meet mine, and she moves, closing the distance between us. She grabs my hand, and a determined look settles over her as she nods.

"Yes. I do."

Chapter Twelve

Brielle

"Yes. I do."

I've known for some time that I trust him more than any sane woman should, but it's the first time I've spoken the confirmation out loud, and it surprises him. His jaw tightens at my words, and he swallows, attempting to control his outward reaction.

"Okay, then." He offers me a small nod, and slides an arm around my waist. "Let's start with the basics."

I pull in a steadying breath as he places the gun in my hold. The handle is textured, the rubber around it patterned, and it's *heavy*. I hadn't anticipated the weight.

"It's loaded, but the safety is on," he explains, and points to a small switch beside my finger. "You can't fire it unless you flick that off."

"O-okay," I stammer.

I'm holding a loaded weapon.

"Wrap your dominant hand around it here" — he shifts my grip, and guides my left hand up — "and brace it with your other like this."

He corrects the position of my fingers, muttering instructions on proper placement, until I'm holding it to his liking. I try to listen, I really do, but the fear pumping through me is making it difficult.

"You're shaking," he murmurs, his hands dropping to my waist. "Relax, Amour."

I sigh, and lower my arms. "I don't think I can do this, Xander."

"You can't relax?" Rhys, who's been listening from the hidden room, pokes his head out with a smirk. "I'm sure I could help."

"That's not what I meant," I grumble.

"Again, you are *not* fucking helping, Blaze." Xander flicks him off and in the same movement, motions for me to retake my position.

Chuckling, Rhys leans against the doorjamb to watch as I lift the weapon. "Would you like some real help then, Beast?"

Xander, ignoring his brother, nudges my feet apart with his own, widening my stance. His hands lift to steady my arms, and when he makes no move to reply, Rhys laughs again.

"I *do* have a few ideas up my sleeve." Rhys flashes me a toothy grin and winks.

"Fuck me," Xander curses. Releasing me, he murmurs for me to stay put and slowly rounds me, inspecting his work. Sighing, he waves Rhys forward. "Well? Let's see these fabulous ideas of yours."

I do my best to hold the correct posture, but as Rhys steps closer, my hands begin to tremble and the barrel of the gun dips. I straighten it, aiming at a cement block across from me, but Rhys shakes his head and holds out his hand.

"You're not going to feel comfortable holding this until you get over your fear, Flower," he notes as I eagerly pass off the weapon.

"I know, I know." I cross my arms, and glare at the black piece of metal in his hand. "I just…how am I supposed to do that?"

His eyes slide to Xander and they share a knowing look, exchanging unspoken words, before he returns the gun to its owner. With free hands, he reaches for me, grabbing my arms and gently tugging me into him.

"First things first, Flower. You've got to relax." He bands an arm around my waist, and dips his chin to kiss me.

I'm only expecting a quick peck, so when his hand slides up to cup the back of my head and his teeth nip at me playfully, I tense.

"Relax," he repeats the order against my lips, and I sigh, caving to the softness of his mouth against mine.

I understand needing to know the knowledge they're attempting to provide me with, but there's no helping the stress and panic that hinder me. It's a fear that's been ingrained into me, one that grows every time I *see* a gun. Kissing isn't going to fix it.

I suppose it won't hurt, either…

"Quit overthinking, Amour." The heat of Xander's words caress the shell of my ear, and then his hand is on my ass, squeezing me.

The thin fabric of the leggings Rhys picked for me to wear do little to dilute the feeling of his skin against mine, and I shiver, biting back a moan.

Oh. A distraction.

I smirk against Rhys mouth and lean into him, allowing the two of them touching me to slowly melt the rigidity that had tensed my spine.

"That's a good girl, Flower," Rhys praises.

I moan, trembling in his hold as his lips move to trail along my jaw and down my neck. My head drops back, allowing him better access, and Xander seizes the opportunity my open mouth provides. His lips capture mine and his tongue pushes into my mouth hungrily, tasting me, *owning* me. I'm not sure what he's done with the gun. I don't know if it's still on his person, or if he's put it away, but as their lips continue exploring me, I realize that I don't fucking *care*. I let them distract me. I let the excitement of them touching me spark and ignite into a flame of desire that burns away my fear.

I give in.

I lose myself to them.

I don't notice that we've moved until Xander's mouth disappears from my own and I'm pressed back against a wall. I gasp, surprised by the gritty texture of the cement that bites into my exposed shoulder, but before I can question the new position, something cold clamps around my wrists.

The chains.

I open my eyes, my heart hammering against my ribs as my arms are lifted above my head and locked into place.

"Yellow and red, Flower." Rhys grazes his teeth over my collar bone and chuckles as I writhe against him.

My safewords.

This isn't the first time we've used restraints but it seems that, despite my obvious enjoyment at being bound, my men are determined to remind me that I'm in charge. I nod my understanding, biting my lip as he trails his hands down my sides and to my waist. He hooks his fingers into my leggings and drags them off legs, hissing when he comes face to face with my pussy.

"So fucking wet, Flower." He growls his appreciation as Xander reappears beside me.

He grabs my chin and kisses me roughly, pressing my body back against the wall as Rhys hooks a hand behind my knee and lifts. He spreads me, opening my legs, and it's only then, as something solid and cold brushes my clit that I realize I *should* have cared about the gun.

"Oh my god." I tug my chin out of Xander's hold and look down, watching in abject horror as the barrel of the gun grinds against my exposed pussy.

"Something wrong, Amour?" Xander chuckles.

"I-I…" I can't speak.

Stunned, I try to close my legs, but with Rhys' hold on my knee, I'm kept firmly in place, allowing the gun to continue its path toward my center.

Oh my god.

I squeak, mortified as my stomach curls with pleasure. It's everything I can do to keep from moaning as the barrel slips between my wet folds, spreading me.

Oh.

My.

God.

"Yellow and red." Rhys reminds me of the colors again as he tugs my tank down, exposing my breasts, but I've become useless putty in their holds.

He pinches my nipple, and sucks the other into his mouth as Xander shifts the weapon forward, grinding it against my sensitive clit. Their lips, their hands, the *gun* between my legs, they're all driving me toward an explosion I'm scared to let detonate. I can't fucking *focus*.

Teeth sink into the swell of my breast, and I jolt, allowing the pain to ground me amidst the downpour of pleasure and panic lancing through me.

Safewords.

I have safewords.

I can stop this if I want to.

Do I want to?

"Yellow and red." My voice is unsteady, but I force the confirmation from my lips. "I trust you. I trust you both."

Xander presses his forehead against my temple, breathing me in as I moan and jerk my hips, grinding my pussy harder against the barrel. "We're going to make you come apart with this gun, Amour."

I groan at his words, and lean into the mounting orgasm beginning to swirl deep within my stomach, allowing it to chase away my fear.

At least for now.

"Don't forget to breathe, Flower," Rhys teases.

Heat creeps up my neck, but I don't have time to focus on the embarrassment attempting to settle on my cheeks. Xander shifts his hold on the gun, and then the muzzle is there, pressing against my center.

"Oh god," I cry out, twisting and tugging at the restraints holding me fast against the wall.

There's a loaded gun pressed against my pussy.

"Last chance, Amour." Xander grabs my face with his free hand, turning me so my eyes meet his.

He's giving me an out. He's allowing me the opportunity to put a stop to this.

My heart is slamming into my ribs, my blood pounding through my skull so loudly it's about all I can hear, but I don't tell him to stop. I kiss him, sealing my fate.

He growls, and slowly, slowly, inches the gun forward. The muzzle spears me first, pushing past my wet folds, and as it enters me, I scream into Xander's mouth. I'm gasping, crying out as the barrel slides into me, painfully at first, until my body adjusts around the foreign object.

I heave, my body waring between panic and pleasure, and Xander waits, allowing me the time I need before he begins to move it, in and out of me.

"Oh, fuck!" I whine, my hips bucking to meet the thrusts of the barrel.

It's terrifying. It's exhilarating. It's sexy and scary and a million other things that overwhelm me as I'm pushed closer to orgasm. It's an excitement only my men can stir within me.

I moan, shifting my legs further apart, and arch my back so my breasts push into Rhys' hold. They continue their ministrations, toying with me until I'm writhing, grinding and begging for release.

"Please, please," I whine, and then it's there, building and crashing into me so hard my entire body convulses.

I think I scream. The raw feeling left behind in my throat is proof of the noise ripping out of me, but I don't hear it. My vision goes white for a moment, the orgasm so intense when paired with terror that I see stars. Xander continues sliding the barrel in and out of me, drawing it out until I slump in the chains, panting, sweating, swearing and crying.

Well.

"That's a good fucking girl, Amour." Xander's praise falls against my sticky skin, and I collapse into his arms as Rhys releases my wrists.

That's one way to face your fears.

Chapter Thirteen

Everett

I'm not sure what I expected to find when Rhys called me home, but finding Brielle chained up and being fucked by a gun was *not* on the list.

"Is this why you wanted me to come back?" I'm standing on the stairs, having just watched Brielle come apart on the barrel of steel and aluminum, with my cock aching in my slacks. "I'll never complain about a show, but you could've mentioned there was no need to panic."

I shoot the last bit at Rhys, who rolls his eyes as he releases Brielle from her restraints.

"Everett," she calls for me, her breathy voice luring me forward like a bug to a flame.

"Hi, pet," I muse, stroking her cheek as Xander places her on unsteady feet.

"You were worried," she murmurs.

It's not a question, and I frown at the understanding that swirls in the depths of her hazel eyes as she reaches for me, still heaving.

She's becoming far too good at reading me.

"I'm all right, pet." I stroke a hand down her back, brushing off her concern.

I'm not willing to admit how fucking torturous my drive home was. When Rhys called, he failed to mention *why* I needed to come back, and I hadn't thought to ask until it was too late. No, I didn't begin to worry until I was trapped in the fucking car with nothing but a wide-open road and my thoughts to keep me company.

What happened? Was David able to recover the deleted security footage? Did Brielle recognize someone in what little video we did have access to? Was there another attack?

The thoughts haunted me until I pulled up in the drive and found the home, seemingly as I'd left it, if not a little cleaner. The panic didn't resurface again until I heard Brielle's screams coming from the basement and found the armory open.

"Do you want to show Everett what you've learned, Amour?" Xander asks.

I look down at her, still shivering and coming down from her climax. She nods, and to my surprise, she reaches for the gun he's holding.

I raise a brow, and look between my brothers.

"She needed to know how to defend herself," Rhys explains.

"Is that what you were doing? Teaching her to defend herself?" I chuckle as Brielle flushes, her movements calculated as she positions her hands on the gun.

"What you saw was just a little exposure therapy," Xander tosses the comment over his shoulder, and I roll my eyes.

"That's the strangest form of exposure therapy I've ever witnessed," I hiss with a smirk.

"Shut the fuck up so she can focus," Xander growls, and nods at Brielle to continue. "Go ahead, Amour."

She widens her stance, and despite being half-naked, she looks stronger, and more confident than I've seen her in weeks. When her arms lift, they're steady, and her eyes narrow, determined, as she locks her sights on the wall across from her.

"You'll want to aim for center mass." I step forward, and gesture to the wall. "The gun will buck once you fire it, so doing that will give you the best chance at hitting your target."

She nods, and glances between the three of us, searching for approval.

"That's good, Amour. Why don't you get dressed, and we'll all go upstairs?" Xander's phone rings, and he glances at me as he grabs it from his pocket. "There might be a lead."

A lead?

He steps away to answer it and I watch with a chuckle as Brielle passes the weapon to Rhys.

"He'll have to clean that before he can use it again." I gesture to the arousal slicking the barrel, and Brielle grimaces.

"I guess it was worth it." She sighs, slipping on her leggings. "Now I'm a double threat." She lifts her tiny fists and shakes them in Rhys and I's direction. "You'd better not cross me."

I laugh, and Rhys clutches at his chest, his hand pressing to his forehead as he feigns swooning. "A woman that can throw a punch *and* shoot a gun? Fuck. How in the hell did we ever find you?"

"Your brothers kidnapped me," she jokes, laughing as I stiffen, surprised.

"What fucking assholes," I grumble, smirking as she crosses toward me and pats my chest.

"Assholes."

The agreement comes from Xander, who's reappeared from his phone call, his blue eyes scanning Brielle as he delicately takes her hand. She's laughing, and it's as the sound echoes through the room around us that his eyes harden, and his jaw sets with regret.

"Amour..." He grits his teeth and looks between the three of us, appearing lost.

The laughter that had filled the room evaporates as if someone's just sucked the oxygen from our lungs, and I tense at the sudden change in atmosphere.

Something's wrong.

A few moments ago when I saw his demeanor darken, I'd believed he was preparing to apologize for taking her, but now...? He's watching her as if she's going to fall apart in his hands, and I know, before he's even opened his mouth, that he's tiptoeing around something that risks shattering her.

"Xander? What is it?" Her quiet voice breaks the silence that's settled in the room, and I tense, unsure of what to expect.

"That was Joe, the head of our security team," he begins, and pauses to look between Rhys and me. The poor fucker's been running around tirelessly trying to help us track down D, but he wouldn't deliver news of such importance — news that would impact Xander like this — via phone call. No, this is something else, and I nod, urging him to continue. "He has a contact at the prison where your father was being held."

I can see a fleeting look of hopefulness cross her face, and my gut wrenches. She's missed the most important part of what he's said.

Was.

"Amour, something's happened."

And then, for the second time today, I watch our woman come apart.

Chapter Fourteen

Brielle

The world is cruel.

I've known that since the moment I watched my mother's life drain out of her body. Hell, I might have even known before then, when I saw her fading from the chemo. Either way, it's been *years* and yet, it still manages to take me by surprise.

Fuck the world.

"Flower?" Rhys strokes a hand down my arm, but I pull away from him.

I'm not ready to cave in to the pain that's wracked my body with broken sobs, tears and snot. I want to be angry, I want to *stay* angry.

It's easier.

"I need to go see him." I force the words past my trembling lips. "I *have* to see him before..."

Before he dies.

It's impossible to ignore the vivid imagery that's playing on repeat in my mind, images of my father, seizing on the floor of his cell, alone and scared. Did he bite off his tongue? Did he vomit and aspirate on it with no one there to put him in the recovery position? God only knows how long the episode lasted. God only knows how long he was unresponsive before someone finally found him and began compressions...

I wince and wrap my arms around myself, attempting to fight off the chill that's seeped into my bones. When will the world stop fucking *taking*? Was it not enough, being a bystander to my mother's death? Now, I have to be the one who decides if my father is going to live or die.

Life support.

It's not a topic my father and I ever broached, although I know my mother had attempted to discuss it with him before her passing. I don't know what came of the conversation, if he decided he'd prefer to live with the help of machines, or if he'd want to slip away into the oblivion, but now *I* have to fucking decide.

This shouldn't be fucking happening.

He shouldn't have been alone. He shouldn't have seized for long enough to stroke out and become unresponsive. All of this...*all of this*...is because of D.

"Yes, you do." I don't anticipate Xander being the one to agree with me, but when he nods and begins to move, I almost collapse in appreciation. "Come on, Amour."

He's paused by the foot of the stairs, waiting for me to pry myself from the spot I've been rooted in, and I sigh, wiping at my face. I look toward Rhys and hold out my hand, sniffling as he takes it gently in his own.

"We've got you, Flower," he murmurs.

Everett gives us space as we make our way toward the steps, and he and Xander follow behind us as we head up them.

"What about the lead you mentioned?" I can hear Everett whisper the question to Xander, and I frown, remembering the reason we'd gone to the basement in the first place.

To prepare.

We'd been waiting for Everett to get home so we could come up with a plan. We were supposed to be making steps toward ending this mess, but now? It's never going to end.

"It's possible that D is some loan shark working with the Wolves. I wanted to go back to that club George was taken from but—"

"You have to go." I tug Rhys to a stop and turn to look between Xander and Everett.

They're watching me carefully, scanning my puffy face and my defeated posture. I know they're worried. I can see it on each of their faces, but we *can't* let this continue. Not if there's a chance at stopping it.

Everett shakes his head. "Not now, pet."

"Yes. Yes, now. If there's a chance..." I trail off, attempting to collect myself as I look between them. "Please. You have to end this. You have to try."

"Your father needs you, Flower," Rhys murmurs.

Guilt and anger swarm me.

All I want is to clean up this mess, to end the hell that my father may have very well created for me, but Rhys is right. My father *needs* me. I've seen the detriment of patients being on their own while they're struggling to survive. He needs someone who loves him in that hospital room with him, even if I'm pissed at him. Even if I don't understand what he's done, or why he's made the decisions that he's made.

I have to go.

"I'll go. I'll be fine on my own. Just drop me off at a bus station and I'll—"

"No, absolutely the fuck not," Xander interrupts, his jaw tense. "You are not going by yourself."

"A crowded hospital is going to be far safer than it is staying here by myself," I press.

"No. I'm not debating this with you, Amour. It's not an option," Xander barks.

I release a rushed breath and wave my hand between them angrily. "Fine. One of you can *escort* me, but the others need to go get answers. I'm done fucking hiding."

I don't expect the laughter that comes from Rhys, or the smirk that curls up Everett's lips. Xander grumbles a curse under his breath, and pinches the bridge of his nose, sighing.

"All right, Amour. You win. We'll divide and conquer, but if we do this, we're doing it *my* way. Deal?" He looks up me, his brow raised.

"Deal."

Chapter Fifteen

Rhys

It's decided with little to no argument which one of us is going to the hospital with Brielle, and once that decision is out of the way, the rest of the plan comes together quickly.

"She is not to be let out of your sight, do you fucking understand me?" Xander has finished giving Joe a rundown, and has moved onto threatening the man. "I don't give two shits if Everett is with her. Do *not* leave her side."

Brielle, who's pulling on one of my hoodies, rolls her eyes.

"Beast," she scolds.

He pauses long enough to glance in her direction before he turns his attention back to threatening Joe. I chuckle at the annoyed expression that twists onto her face and wrap an arm around her so I can lead her back toward the door.

"You'd better leave him to it, Flower," I murmur, pressing a kiss to the top of her head.

"He's worrying himself over nothing. This D guy isn't stupid enough to show up at the hospital," she hisses.

"Let him worry, Flower. That's how he shows he cares." I force a smile onto my lips and cup her face. Tracing my thumb over her bottom lip, I lift her chin so I can meet her gaze. "Promise me you'll be safe, Flower."

"I'll be fine, I promise." She stretches up onto her toes and presses a quick kiss to my lips as Everett reappears from the basement. Eyeing him, she whispers, "I know better than to be reckless."

I chuckle, remembering my brother's previous choices of punishment, and nod.

"Besides, it should really be *me* worrying about *you* two." She glances toward Xander and sighs. "You'll be careful, won't you?"

"We always are," I assure her.

"Rhys." Xander, seeming to be finished with his harassment of Joe, gestures toward the garage. "We should get going."

I pull Brielle into my chest and hug her tightly. Releasing her, I watch reluctantly as she crosses the room toward Xander. She jabs a finger in his chest, and as she begins berating him, Everett steps up to me.

"She loves you." It's not a question, and as I meet his gaze, his jaw sets firmly. "Don't do anything stupid. She needs you to come back in one piece."

"I'll do anything for her."

* * * *

We've picked a good time to come back to the bar.

It looks like, despite the happy hour sign flashing in the window, the place is nearly devoid of customers, with only one car in the front lot and two around the back. It's slow enough that one of their dancers, an older woman in skimpy clothes that reveal far too many wrinkles, is leaning against the front of the building, heating her drug of choice in a glass pipe. She doesn't appear to be in a hurry to get back inside, which means there's not enough money floating around within the shitty walls behind her to keep the workers busy.

"No security?" It's the second time Xander's voiced the question, and again, I nod, gesturing toward the doors.

"The cheap fucks don't even have a bouncer for the girls," I confirm.

He glances over his shoulder at our three lackeys sitting in the backseat, eyeing each of them carefully before he turns back to face the steering wheel.

Rolling his neck, he cracks it, releasing some of the pent-up tension before he speaks. "If they don't have any hired muscle, the bartender is likely armed."

"One of them should go around the back to guard the rear door. We don't want anyone leaving before the party's over," I mutter.

"You heard him." Xander holds up a finger, and the men murmur their understanding as he pushes his door open. "Rhys, I want you on my six."

I nod and slip from the car to follow him, smirking as our sudden appearance makes the woman drop her pipe. Her eyes are wide with recognition, and a moment of fear slips past her carefully curated mask before she stills and settles back against the wall. She makes no move to rush inside to warn her comrades, and I can't decide if that makes her smart or selfish. *Maybe both.*

"Is the kid here?" I bark the question, and she jumps, surprised to have us addressing her.

"K-kid?" she asks.

I'd warned Beast on the drive over that during our last visit there'd been a teenager working in the back. He was the only reason Everett and I hadn't caused more damage than we did. Unfortunately, his presence tonight isn't going to change what's coming.

I just want to be prepared.

"Roy." At the sound of the kid's name, the woman shakes her head.

"He ain't here." She juts her chin toward the street and raises a brow. "I ain't here either?"

She's asking for permission to leave, and as soon as Xander waves her off, she takes her chance. She darts forward, disappearing into the dark, and I chuckle, leaning close to him.

"The Beast is getting soft," I hiss, low enough that the two men behind me won't hear.

"You only have one person to blame for that," he mutters, and tries his best to disguise the smirk that lifts up the corner of his lips. Shaking his head, he nods toward the doors. "Let's go in there and finish this for her."

Chapter Sixteen

Brielle

The hospital is crowded.

It's the first time I've set foot in a clinical setting since my working interview, and I'd almost forgotten the sheer volume of people these buildings can hold. It should be comforting, this is my element after all, *this* is what I trained for, but I can't ignore the tightness beginning to settle in my chest. I'm on edge, and Everett notices.

"You'll be with him soon, pet," he murmurs, stroking a hand down my back.

I lean against him with a small nod and scour the people who're waiting ahead of us in line for the elevators, unsure if I'm *ready* to see him. It was hard enough, seeing my mother hooked up to tubes and medications when I had no concept of their purposes. Now, with a nursing degree under my belt, when I walk into my father's room, I'll understand what every single wire, machine, tube and monitor is doing. I'll know the statistics of surviving *without* all of it, and I'm going to have to decide whether or not to let him try.

"Conrad will meet us outside of the unit to escort us back," Joe states. His contact from the prison, who escorted my father over in the ambulance, has been placed in charge of guarding his room. He's guaranteed us a few minutes with him, but he's made it clear that even *that* much is pushing our luck. "He doesn't think there'll be enough time to meet with a physician."

"Not now." Everett shakes his head, and I frown.

"I'm not going to be allowed to talk with one of the doctors?" I blanch, my head spinning. "B-but I have so many questions. Do we know his level of brain activity? What percentage of the bleed were they able to—"

"Brielle." Everett squeezes my hand and tugs me forward as the family ahead of us files into the elevator. "One step at a time, pet. Let's just focus on seeing him for now, okay?"

I bite my lip and look between him and Joe, defeated. "O-okay…"

"No one is expecting you to make any decisions today. I'm sure Xander can call and work something out with the hospital, and then we'll come back as often as you need," he assures me.

I nod, grateful to have at least the semblance of a plan in place as we step into the elevator.

I don't have to decide today.

I try to hold onto that feeling as we rise to the fifteenth floor, but it's difficult not to be refueled by anger and guilt as we exit the elevator. Conrad is waiting for us as promised, his standard uniformed pressed to a perfection that indicates on obvious lack of labor. It irritates me, knowing that he accompanied my *dying* father to the hospital, and did next to nothing to help keep him alive.

"You his daughter?" Conrad questions, his eyes scanning over me skeptically.

I nod, chewing on the inside of my cheek as a scowl tugs onto the man's wrinkled face. "Yes."

He doesn't look impressed, and I shift uncomfortably under his steely gaze as he continues scrutinizing me.

What is his problem?

"So...George?" Everett prompts, and steps in front of me enough to break the man's unwavering line of sight.

Conrad grumbles something under his breath and jabs a thumb over his shoulder toward a set of glass doors. "He's through here."

He turns and swipes a badge over the card reader next to the entrance, pausing a beat until a small buzz sounds before tugging the door open. He doesn't wait to make sure we're following him, and I glance up at Everett, suddenly unsure.

"It's all right, pet," he murmurs, motioning for me to go ahead of him.

I sigh and start in the direction Conrad's headed off in, passing a nurses' station and numerous rooms with intubated patients. I wrap my arms around myself, hating the sight of the men and women lying lifeless in their beds, their machines creating a symphony of life-saving measures that seeps into the open space.

"This way," Conrad calls over his shoulder, and turns down a hall marked *Quarantine*.

"Why is he in isolation?" I glance at Everett, my heart leaping into my chest.

He opens his mouth, but before he can reply, Conrad's nonchalant response filters into the hall. "He's a prisoner. It's protocol."

I stall, my teeth grinding together. Even here, while hospitalized and struggling to survive, he's being kept separated from other people.

"Everett, I—"

"We'll figure it out, pet." His jaw is tight, and I can see the contempt on his face as he watches Conrad lower himself into a flimsy chair.

I do my best to ignore the tears threatening to form, my anger boiling as the guard stations himself just outside door. Aside from a single nurse hovering at a nearby computer, and Conrad, this hall is empty and dark.

He deserves better than this.

"Come on, pet." Everett's hand brushes my back, urging me forward, and slowly, my feet comply with the demand.

Shuffling, I wring my hands and try my best to steady my breathing. Before, when my mother had been in the hospital, it'd been easy to feign bravery for Sammy. Now, with him missing, and my mother gone, and my father dying, the only person I have left to be brave for is *me*.

How can I be strong for myself?

I feel lost. So overwhelmingly *lost*.

"I'm here, Brielle."

With Everett's comforting words as an anchor amidst the onslaught of emotions swarming me, I swallow my fear, and round the corner into the room.

I will be strong.

For me.

Chapter Seventeen

Xander

Walking into the shitty building, it's easy to picture how my life could have turned out if not for my brothers. The Beast was created to rule an empire of businesses like this one, establishments run on the backs of broken women and drunken bastards too lost to save themselves. My father believed it best to line his pockets with easy money, money *he* didn't need to work for. He tore down men and women that stood in his way, and taught me to do the same. If it wasn't strip clubs, it was peddling weapons. If it wasn't illegal firearms, it was drugs, and eventually, when that wasn't enough, it was women.

I burned those bridges down while my father's body was still fucking warm. My brothers helped me realize what I wanted the Grimm name to stand for, and while it's still not respectable, it sure as fuck isn't what it could have been. What it *would* have been, if not for them.

I'm watching Rhys now. He's taken up residence on one of the iron barstools, his lighter laid on the countertop in front of him, a silent reminder of his namesake.

"Beast. Blaze." The guy behind the counter, who eyes us warily, has seen better days. There's a fading bruise circling his left eye, and beneath a rotting-looking bandage covering his lower arm, I suspect a burn is festering. "I don't have any new information for you."

I step up beside my brother and drag my eyes around the dimly lit room. There's one man sitting near the stage, but he's too drunk to keep his attention on the woman swinging her hips in front of him. While he doesn't pose an immediate risk, I'm still not willing to take any chances.

I flick my hand and the two men I brought with us disperse, moving to guard the possible exits. Once they've taken their positions, I lower myself on to the stool beside Rhys, and smirk.

"I think you've been holding out on us." I follow the man's gaze as it dips momentarily to something hiding behind the counter.

I slide my gun free of its holster as he begins to move toward it, switching off the safety and aiming it between his eyes. He freezes when he clocks the weapon pointed at his head, and curses, his teeth grinding together.

"What kind of surprise do you have back there for us?" I jut my chin forward, and Rhys stands.

He reaches behind the counter and laughs as he pulls a baseball bat free. "You thought this would be enough to stop us?"

He passes the bat to me, and I roll my eyes, setting my own weapon aside so I can twist it in my hand, inspecting it. The weapon he'd been ready to wield against us is wood, not steel, and has been sleeved with a tube sock to keep the victim from snatching it away. It's fucking laughable, and for some reason, it angers me more than a fucking gun would have.

"Just don't burn me again...please." He groans.

"Getting burned will be the least of your fucking problems if you lie to me or my brother again." I snap my hand forward and latch onto the man's arm. Before he has a chance to react, I haul him toward me and force his palm flat against the bar top. "Your back room."

He tries to rip himself free, but doesn't become desperate until I pull out my knife. Once he sees the serrated steel, he jerks and drops, attempting to get his hand loose.

"What about it?" He screams the question, and Rhys holds down the man's other arm to keep him restrained in the position I want.

"I want the name of the usurer you rent it out to." I raise a brow, annoyance filling me as he shakes his head.

"I-I don't know him. I only ever spoke with Lincoln." He tries, but I press the tip of the blade into the back of his hand.

"You're *lying* to me." I shout.

"No! No. Lincoln never told me the guy's name—"

"We know he came in the front door. You've seen him around enough to give us a vague description."

Rhys growls, tightening his hold as the bartender writhes in our grasp.

I press the knife forward, just a fraction of an inch, but it's enough to pierce his skin. Blood beads around the blade, and as the guy moves, it digs further into his flesh.

"That's all I know, I swear." He's shouting, cursing, but I can see the lie hiding behind his eyes.

There's something more. Something he's unwilling to share.

"You're going to tell me who he is." I grin as he shakes his head, and pull the knife free.

He looks relieved for a moment, his eyes darting to his hand, and while his gaze is locked on his bleeding skin, I plunge the knife through his flesh and bone. He screams, but with his hand now secured to the bar top, there's nowhere for him to go. He twists and yanks, but his movements only cause further damage.

I chuckle as he realizes it's pointless to fight his situation, and lean closer to him as his screams dampen down to soft, pathetic whimpers.

"I want a fucking name," I spit.

"Or what?" Sweat beads on his forehead, but he lifts his chin, attempting to remain defiant.

I laugh at his reaction, and glance toward Rhys, who's pulling his own switchblade free.

"Blaze?" I ask.

His eyes light with fire, and he smirks as he drags the blade of his knife over the joint of one of the man's outstretched digits.

"Or…" With little pressure, he slices, and the blade hacks off the man's index finger.

He wails, and starts flailing his free arm wildly in a desperate attempt to stop us.

"We'll take off all ten."

Chapter Eighteen

Brielle

The man lying in the hospital bed before me doesn't look like my father.

His normally rounded cheeks have become concave, and his previously average frame has turned skeletal, deteriorated by the drugs I know had been forced into his system. He's a ghost of the man I'd traded my life for a few short months ago, and the realization is almost enough to take me to my knees.

"Oh, Dad..." I whisper as I move into the room.

Tubes, wires, monitors and IV lines surround him, but unlike I'd anticipated, it's not the sight of those that bother me. No, what bothers me is the shiny silver handcuff that locks his limp wrist to the bedrail, tight enough to cause visible irritation. I glare over my shoulder at Conrad, who's moved the chair enough to see into the room without having to stand, and gesture at the cuffs.

"Are these really necessary?" I ask, attempting to dampen the angry flame that's sparked to life in my chest.

"It's protocol." The simplistic response, and the nonchalant shrug of his shoulders, make an annoyed curse hiss through my clenched teeth.

"He's *unconscious*."

"Pet." Everett squeezes my shoulder, and I force in a deep breath, allowing his touch to ground me.

I *need* to remember the reason we're here, but it's impossible to ignore the unjust conditions my father is being kept in.

"This shouldn't be happening..." I whisper.

D did this.

I drag my gaze over the shattered man lying in front of me, my eyes logging every bump, scratch and bruise that decorates his body. His head is bandaged from the surgery to stop the bleeding in his brain, and the intubation tube hangs crooked from his dry lips. Track marks litter the inside of his exposed arm, and bruises darken his pale skin.

The pain he must have endured...

I reach for him, hesitant. While I know touching him won't hurt him physically, there's a piece of me that still burns with resentment over what he's done, and I'm worried he'll sense that bitterness. If what we think he's done is true...how can I forgive the hell that he's caused for me?

For everyone?

He's my father.

Biting my lip, I reach forward and gently straighten the blanket covering his chest.

"I'm here, Dad," I murmur. "It's Bri."

A lump forms in my throat at the use of my family's nickname for me, and tears sting my eyes. All of the anger, all of the strength I'd mustered to come into this room, disappears, leaving nothing but grief and sadness in its wake. My knees tremble, and I lean against Everett, trusting him to support my weight as I struggle to remain standing.

He holds me without complaint and cradles me to his side, allowing me the time I need to cry about the uncertainty of the future. I can't fathom what will happen to my family without my father, or how I'll explain his death to Samuel. I don't know where we'll go, or how I'll afford to support us both.

"It's going to be okay, Dad." I step forward and squeeze his hand. "You're going to be okay."

I'm not sure if he can hear me, or if he's too far gone to know who I am, but I press on, continuing to murmur words of encouragement in the hope that somehow they're reaching him. If not here, in this room, then in the universe wherever he may be.

"I don't want you to worry about Sammy and me, okay? We're going to be fine. We're going to figure this out." I swipe away my tears and pray that, if he *can* hear me, that he can't tell I'm lying.

I've never been good at lying.

"Brass," Joe calls from the doorway, and I know before either of them have said anything more, that my time is up.

We have to go.

"I love you a-and I forgive you, Dad." My voice cracks and my chest aches as I lean over him.

It's as I'm pressing my lips to his cool forehead that Conrad appears beside us and grabs me by the shoulder.

"I said your time was up," he barks.

"Do *not* fucking touch her." Everett is quick to round me, his hand shoving into Conrad's chest hard enough that the man stumbles backward, releasing me.

Tension fizzles and snaps through the air like a live wire has just touched the floor. I don't breathe, afraid that doing so will snap whatever shred of control the two men have left as they size one another up.

"Brielle." Joe is hovering by the door, one hand reaching for the pistol I know is concealed at his waist, while the other stretches toward me.

I don't move.

"Brielle, why don't you go wait in the hall with Joe? I need a moment to speak with Conrad, *alone*." Everett's jaw ticks as he nudges me toward Joe's outstretched hand.

My stomach drops. "Everett, wait, please—"

"It's all right, Brielle." He drops his gaze from the guard in front of him, just long enough to offer me a comforting smile. "I love you. I'll be right there."

I gape, too overwhelmed to get the words out as Joe takes my wrist and tugs me away from them both. It's not until he's closing the door that the sentence tumbles free, and I can only hope it reaches him before he's managed to seal it shut.

"I love you, too."

Chapter Nineteen

Everett

"I love you, too."

Her words echo through the room and I smile, despite the guard closing in on me.

I've known for some time now, the feeling that fills me every time I'm near her. I've been ignoring it, pushing it to the back of my brain since the night that she chose to stay in our home, even though it risked her life. It was a risk she took for *us* and it stuck with me.

It grew.

It grew until I could no longer ignore it, the feeling so insistent and tormenting that I allowed to spread within me. Until it felt like every breath I took was for her. Seeing her here, watching her mourn her father, and whisper those words to him for what could be the last time, stirs a realization through my gut. They're too important, those fucking words. Too crucial to hide.

I had to say them.

She needed to hear them.

And now, with them still hanging in the air, I turn my attention back to Conrad, scowling.

"What the fuck is your problem?" I try to keep my voice low. It'll be better if we don't cause a commotion in a fucking hospital, but I can't let this piece of shit off the hook. He's been nothing short of asinine and disrespectful to Brielle our entire time here, a transgression I was already struggling to overlook. I draw the line at him putting his hands on her. "She's grieving. Where the fuck is your compassion?"

"Compassion? Her father's a drugged-out felon. She doesn't deserve my *compassion*." He spits, cursing as I grab him by the shirt collar.

"You owe her a goddamned apology," I growl, heat rising in my chest.

He will learn to treat our woman with the respect she deserves, or fucking else. She holds my entire world in her hand, and I'll be damned if he's going to walk all over her like she's some fucking doormat.

"I don't owe her shit." He shoves at me, but I hold him firm.

"You are going to regret how you've acted toward my woman tonight, Conrad," I threaten.

He smirks. "Rose isn't yours."

I'm so surprised, so taken aback by his use of that godforsaken nickname, that I'm not prepared for the pain that crashes through my temple. I fall to the floor, stunned, as my eyes roll over the gun he's just used to strike me down.

"She was *never* yours."

His words follow me as I slip unwillingly toward an all-consuming darkness.

No.

Brielle…
Fuck!
And then the ground opens up and swallows me whole.

Chapter Twenty

Brielle

I love you.

The words I'd been so afraid to share with him, with a man who stole me from my home, now bubble in my chest and rise in my throat, desperate to escape.

I love him.

I love him so much that the mere thought of him not knowing for one second longer *hurts.* I have to tell him. I want to scream it from the rooftops.

"Please, Joe." I pause, mid-stride, and turn on my heel to face the man who's planted himself firmly in front of my father's door. "Please let me in."

He shakes his head, unwilling to budge, and I curse, my hands wringing through my hair as I begin pacing again. It's not fair. It's my fault that Conrad got pissed off. Everett shouldn't be in there, fighting my battles for me.

But...

They've all been doing that for some time, now. The Grimm Brothers, my men, whom I'm not sure I'll be able to survive without once this is over. They've changed me, morphed the naive girl that I was into a smarter, hardened puzzle piece that doesn't make sense without three other pieces holding it together.

They're mine, as much as I am theirs.

Footsteps sound against the tile, and I stiffen, my gaze lifting from the floor to inspect the noise. I expect to see a nurse, or if I'm lucky, a physician I can distract with questions about my father's condition. What I don't expect to see is a man, dressed in slacks and a button down, heading in our direction. He looks disheveled in a way that only someone struggling to hold their life together can, and I frown, understanding that look all too well.

It's how I looked when my mother died.

It's how I'm sure I look now.

This man just hasn't realized yet, that no matter how nice you dress, no matter how put together you appear, you'll still feel shattered on the inside.

He must be here with someone.

I eye the other rooms in the hall, wondering if I hadn't noticed someone in my haste to keep up with Conrad, but they're all dark.

Maybe he took a wrong turn?

I glance at the man again, and offer him a sympathetic smile. He's almost reached my father's room, and there's nothing else down here aside from a fire exit.

He must need some air.

Something inside my father's room crashes, and I jump, whirling toward the door as Joe moves to open it. I'm so distracted, so caught off guard by the noise, that I almost don't hear the man when he speaks.

"How's your father?"

His voice stalls me, a chill racing up my spine as panic stalls my heart in my chest.

I know that voice.

I can't breathe, my entire body going numb as I lift my eyes to his face, bewildered.

I realize too late that I recognize his eyes.

The eyes of the masked man that murdered Lincoln.

The eyes of the man destroying my family.

It's...

"D."

Draven

I watch the recognition cross her face. The fear, the panic, the *anger* that morphs into shock as I pull my weapon free from my waistband.

"D." She chokes out the initial, and I smile, straightening my shoulders as her wide eyes scan me.

I'm proud to be seen by her, *truly* seen, for the first time, and I step forward, overwhelmed by the need sudden need to touch her. "Hello, Rose."

She stumbles backward and the man in the doorway pivots, his attention torn between me and Conrad, who's moved to block the way into George's open room.

"Everett."

The unconscious Grimm Brother is visible, lying just out of reach on the hospital floor, and I laugh at the panic that lances through her voice as she calls for him again.

"Everett!"

Their head of security twitches, his hand wrapping around the handle of a gun sheathed at his waist, and I shake my head, barking, "Don't be stupid."

He grits his teeth but releases the weapon, his arms slow as they raise in silent surrender.

"Get behind me, Brielle," he whispers.

"No." I shift my aim, pointing the barrel of my silencer at his chest as I step forward. "She's coming with me."

He grabs her arm, prepared to put himself between us, and I react, my anger blinding me. A pop echoes through the hall as I pull the trigger, firing a bullet from the silencer, and Rose screams as it strikes him. It tears into his shoulder, knocking him back, and blood rushes from the wound.

"Joe!" She yelps, but with him and the Grimm Brother disarmed, there's no one left to keep her from me.

I lunge forward and grab her by the hair, pulling tight enough to force her away from Joe as he grasps at the air where she'd just been, desperate to keep her from me.

"Please, please." Her hand wraps around mine, clawing at my skin, but I hold her tight.

"We are going home," I mutter and retake my aim, centering the barrel between the man's wide eyes as he struggles to catch his breath. "Do not move."

He inches forward with his hand pressed to his wound, ignoring me, and behind him, I can see the Grimm Brother beginning to twitch.

It's now or never.

"We are going *home*," I repeat, and pull the trigger.

Brielle

Joe's mouth hangs open, but no sound escapes as he stumbles toward us — toward *me* — determined.

"We are going *home*." The repeated growl is a death sentence, as D fires his weapon again.

A silent *click* registers in my ears, and then a bullet rockets into Joe's stomach, knocking him to his knees. He sputters as he collapses and fresh blood pours like a river from the wound as his head bounces off the tile with a sickening thud. He doesn't move, and my stomach coils as bile burns the back of my throat.

Is he...?

"Joe," I croak, my throat tight with a scream I refuse to let escape as I'm hauled back toward the stairs.

My head is reeling, my scalp burning as he tugs relentlessly at my strands, but he doesn't pause, not even when a nurse screams from down the hall.

"Brielle..." The groan follows me as D forces me into the stairwell, and I yelp as he presses the barrel of the gun against my temple.

"Move!" There's urgency in his voice, and with a loaded weapon—wielded by an unpredictable man—pressed against my head, I have no choice but to comply.

I clumsily descend the stairs, panic clawing through my chest.

Everett.

Joe...

I'm sorry.

Chapter Twenty-One

Rhys

I settle back into the passenger seat, feeling far too giddy for a man that just cut off six fingers.

Fuck, was it worth it, though.

We have a name.

"Draven Augustin," Xander spits, and typing crackles over the car speakers as David, his hacker, audibly types something on his end of the call.

"Addresses are supposed to be public record, but with his status, it's been concealed." David curses, and Xander grips the steering wheel tighter, before the man on the other end laughs. "Ha! Tech genius my ass. I've got it."

"Send it to me," Xander barks.

"I'm on it, Beast," David confirms, and the call disconnects.

I bounce in my seat, excited. "Let me burn down his mansion."

"Jesus, Rhys, not now." Xander rolls his eyes, and his phone pings as the address comes through via text. "Call Everett. Tell them to get back to the house, now."

I pull my cell free from my pocket, and as I unlock it to dial out, a call comes through, lighting up the screen.

"Speak of the devil." I hit accept and put the phone on speaker. "Everett, have we got some great fucking news for —"

"She's gone." The whispered interruption cracks my chest wide open.

The air rushes from my lungs, and suddenly I'm suffocating.

"W-What?" I choke.

I can't breathe without her.

The tires screech and the car jolts to a stop as Xander maneuvers us onto the shoulder, cursing. "This fucker is always one step ahead of us. *One* fucking step."

I can't live without her.

"It's Draven Augustin. That self-made billionaire who grew up in the city. Joe gave me the name before..." Everett takes a deep breath and sighs. "Before he died."

He killed Joe.

"Can you drive?" Xander pulls back onto the road and presses the gas to the floorboard, lurching the car forward.

"You think a fucking concussion is going to stop me? What's the plan?" Everett asks.

Xander reaches over and squeezes my shoulder, the comforting gesture so out of character for him, it forces me out of my haywire thoughts.

"We're going to get her back," I state.

Chapter Twenty-Two

Brielle

"Rose."

I jump, startled by the nearness of his voice as I fall out of my thoughts. Blinking, my eyes jolt to the open door where D is crouched, watching me.

I lost track of time.

The car that I'd been forced into has stopped, and behind him stands a house so large I feel like it could swallow the entire world whole.

Where are we?

"It's been a messy business getting you here, but it's over with now. You're home." He reaches out, offering me his hand, but I shy away from it.

After everything he's done, after all the pain and destruction he's caused, what else does he expect?

He rolls his eyes and sighs as if I've disappointed him before taking a step back, allowing me the space I need to exit the vehicle. I hesitate, scanning the world outside the windows in the hopes that I'll spot a way to escape. Maybe a person willing to help, or a neighboring house that could shield me should he open fire, but there's nothing. Just rolling acres of grass, and a metal fence in the distance.

"Rose, come." He snaps his fingers as if I'm nothing more than a dog, and wags the gun in the doorway, a silent threat for my compliance.

I have no other options.

Gritting my teeth, I slowly slide from the town car, my heart hammering in my ears. I'm on edge, my body coiled with fear as I glare at the weapon in his grasp.

"Come on, let's get you settled." He motions forward, and my gaze follows the path up to the front door.

Survive.

Survive until they come for you.

I pull in a small breath and bite my tongue to keep from commenting on the psychotic idea that I will *settle* into this house with him. It's insane, thinking that I'll be happy here, when the only thing I can see when I look at him is the destruction he's caused. *The death.* He's unpredictable, and I can't risk angering him.

With no other alternatives, I cave and start up the cement pavers to the front door. He murmurs something under his breath, praise I think, but my blood is pumping too loudly in my ears for me to hear him. I'm trembling, fear skating up my spine as my reality closes in on me. There's no one standing between me and D any longer, and as long as he continues wielding his weapon, I'm completely at his mercy. My eyes prick with tears at the thought, and I wince as he steps up beside me to unlock the door. He presses his thumb against the doorhandle, and a mechanical whizz sounds as it unlocks at the scan of his fingerprint. Pushing open the door, his teeth flash in a perfect, toothy grin as he turns to me.

"Welcome home, Rose." His happy smile makes my stomach curl, and bile burns the back of my throat as I hesitantly cross into the foyer.

It's dark, but as I enter the house, he flips a switch, illuminating the rooms and the photos that surround me. Frame after frame of pictures hang in neat, orderly lines on the walls. Some in black and white. Some in color. All of...*me*.

Oh my god.

The room tilts on its axis and my legs turn molten beneath me, making me stumble. I can't catch my balance, and through the fog of panic I realize I'm going to faint as I collapse, my eyes rolling back. I'm too far gone to feel the ground as I crash against it, my blood pressure bottoming out and a black curtain sweeping over my vision. Unable to fight it, I freefall into a void of darkness.

Please...hurry.

* * * *

The memories assault me before I'm fully awake. Memories of Everett lying unconscious on the floor, of Joe's blood staining the white hospital linoleum. Of my face, photographed and hanging on every inch of visible wall space in the foyer...

I don't want to open my eyes.

I want it all to have been a dream, but as I stretch out my arms, desperate to find one of my men lying beside me, I'm met with the cold truth of my reality. I'm alone, and there is no waking up from this nightmare.

Grimacing, I sit up and quickly scan the room. I appear to be alone, and in a bedroom — *his* bedroom, if the smell of the sheets beneath me is any indication. I scramble to get off the bed, the feeling of my bare feet hitting the cold hardwood floor enough to make me shiver.

He took my shoes.

It's laughable, the idea that making me barefoot would stop me from running if I thought I had any real opportunity at escaping. Asshole. I roll my eyes and glance around, trying to gauge my surroundings. It's dark, and either late or early enough in the day that no light comes from behind the drawn curtains. I can make out the outline of some furniture that's scattered throughout the room, and along the far walls there are three separate doors. One must be the way out, but which one?

There's only one way to find out.

I cross the room, my feet light beneath me, but I pause when I spot the artwork hanging across from the bed. It's *huge*, and from the silhouette I can barely make out, the person the picture is portraying is feminine. After seeing the entrance of the house, I can only be led to one conclusion, and it makes my heart rate spike again as disgust wrings my cut. It's another picture of me, it has to be.

I lurch forward, stomach rolling, and flip on the light, desperate to see it. If this picture is here, behind closed doors, in his *bedroom* of all places, I can only imagine what it's depicting.

When I finally swallow my fear and look up, I'm not prepared for the face that stares back at me, immortalized by paint and canvas. It's...

"Mom...?"

Chapter Twenty-Three

Draven

"There are only a few of us that have trained in combat. I'm really not sure—"

"I've run the numbers. Even if they bring what little security detail they have left, we still outnumber them," I interrupt with a stiff wave of my hand.

Conrad is pacing in front of the monitors that fill the wall, re-running my plan over and over in his tiny little head. His lips are downturned, and I can see the distaste that's settled onto his face, but I'm too preoccupied to care.

Rose is awake.

I'm watching the live security feed of our room, smirking as she jumps down from the bed to inspect the space she's woken up in. Her hesitation is noticeable, but I allow her the time she needs to explore, hoping that she'll find that the room is to her liking. If not, I suppose she'll have to get used to it.

"Do the others know who we're going up against?" Conrad stops in front of the screens, and I grunt as he blocks my view of Rose.

"They stopped caring once I waved a thick stack of cash under their noses." I shrug.

"You'd better hope they're not anticipating a fight. If they come armed, we will not win," he mutters and starts toward the door, cursing.

"Tell the others to get ready. I'm sure they're already on the way," I call after him, shaking my head as my attention returns to the security feed.

Rose has moved and light now fills the room. She's looking up toward one wall, and I know without changing the camera angle that she's found the portrait of her mother.

I suppose it's time we had a little chat.

Standing from the chair, I move toward the steel door of my security room, smiling.

Finally.

I'm going to have her all to myself.

* * * *

Brielle

"Mom…?"

Her smile, something that I've missed since the day she passed, now haunts me as I retreat, backing up until my legs hit the bed. She's young in the picture, and missing the signature streak of gray hair that had framed her face before radiation fried it from her scalp. We could be identical if not for the hazel eyes I inherited from my father.

What is this picture doing here?

She's posed with her face angled up, her hands clutched in her lap holding…

A rose.

Her favorite flower.

My mind reels, and I have to sit down on the edge of the bed, too unsteady to remain standing.

What the fuck is going on?

I can't breathe, my lungs constrict as if barbed wire has been wrapped around them, making it impossible to pull in a satisfying breath. Tears stream down my face, and I can't tug my gaze away from the unsettling photograph.

Oh, Mom…

"I don't understand." I wrap my arms around myself, and do my best to regain control of my breathing.

One.

Two.

Three…

I count, desperate to stay focused, and use the other techniques my men have shown me to stay grounded.

Keep calm, Brielle.

They're coming.

The reminder does little to settle the erratic pounding of my heart. Something clicks from across the room, and I snap my attention toward the noise as one of the doors swings open. D enters the room, and I stand, involuntarily searching him for his gun.

I don't see it.

"I think it's time we talked, Rose." He offers me a kind smile, and it's as I watch him cross the room that I realize that I recognize him.

"Draven. Draven Augustin," I whisper damningly, and he nods, his smile growing.

"Yes, Rose," he confirms.

Draven Augustin.

Draven *fucking* Augustin.

The man is a self-made billionaire who went to school in our city. His face is plastered on every billboard within a fifty-mile radius, boasting of some new technology he's created to make lives easier. Almost every woman I know is obsessed with him.

What the fuck does he want with me?

"Why don't you take a look at this?" He holds something out for me, and I scan the object in his hands, confused.

"A yearbook...?" I don't make any move to take it from him.

My lips are twisted, caught somewhere between a grimace and a scowl as I eye the leather cover held out toward me.

"Mine." He nods and closes the remaining distance between us. "And your mother's."

My mother's.

He went to school with my mom?

"She never mentioned you." The words slip from me freely before I can stop them, and he grits his teeth, wincing.

"Take it!" he shouts, angered by my words, and I jump, quickly accepting the book from him.

Survive.

I frown and look down at the golden numbers imprinted onto the cover, knowing that I'll have to tread carefully if I want to keep him calm and talking.

"I'm sorry," I apologize, and trace my finger over the year. "You...graduated with my mom?"

He nods, and comes to stand beside me, reaching out to open it. His name is scribbled across the front endpaper, and decorated across the first page are signatures from his classmates along with a few written well wishes. I can see my mother's familiar scrawl, and I quickly read the words.

I'll miss you.

I freeze as his arm wraps around my waist, tugging me against him. "We had to go our separate ways for college."

He flicks to the back of the book and stops on a well-worn page, the corners ripped and faded from years of use. On it, is the original photo of my mother — the one memorialized on the wall — and one of them, cuddled close, with the text *'cutest couple'* typed below it.

They were together?

I tug out of his grasp and shove the book back into his hands, unable to control my budding anger. All this destruction and pain, for *what?*

"Rose." He reaches for me, but I smack away his hands.

"Don't touch me." I shake my head and wrap my arms around myself as everything falls into place. *None of this is my father's fault. All of this...* "Why are you doing this? My mother is *dead.* Is this some sick way of punishing her for falling in love with my dad? Do you really hate her that—"

"I loved your mother!" he yells. He storms forward, closing the distance I've created, and grabs my shoulders roughly, his spit flying in my face as he continues. "I *loved* her. I loved her more than George ever could. He couldn't take care of her, Rose! He couldn't afford to help her when she got sick. I paid for it all, and she *still* didn't want me!"

He shakes me, hard enough that my head snaps back and forth. I whimper, trying to push him away, but his grip is unwavering.

"I couldn't have her, but I will have *you*." He shoves me backward, and I crash to the ground, a screech ripping from my lips. "Your mother couldn't see what we had, but I've been given a second chance with you, Rose."

His body is on mine before I have enough purchase to stand, pinning me to the cold, unforgiving floor.

"We'll be happy together. You'll learn to love me the way she should have." He's rambling as I scream, ignoring my fists as they slam against his chest. "I love you, Rose."

I sob, tears streaming down my face as he straddles my waist and pins my wrists by my sides.

"I love you." He leans forward, and drags his nose along my wet cheek, inhaling deeply. "I love *you*."

I don't anticipate the harsh laughter that comes from my throat as he gently kisses me. The sound stalls him, and he pulls back enough to study me, distracted from his assault.

"I will *never* love you, Draven. I love them. I love the Grimm Brothers."

My words snap whatever threads remain of his sanity.

Chapter Twenty-Four

Draven

"I love the Grimm Brothers."

The words replay over and over in my head as I stare at her, watching the tears roll down her face.

My Rose...

"What have they done to you?"

I can't stop the assault of images that flood my brain. Images of her beneath them, writhing in ecstasy and pleasure as she screams *their* names.

My Rose...

They've altered her.

Tainted her.

Ruined her.

Her lips curl upward in a wicked, sultry smile, and I bite back a shout at the confirmation that look has just provided.

No...

No, my Rose...

I can physically feel something inside me shatter as every dream, every hope I've clung to for the past six years falls apart. She's undone it with one look. She's undone it with three words.

I love them.

It taunts me, echoing through my head like some sick mantra created specifically to torture me, and I yell in her face, desperate to drown them out.

"No. No. No, Rose!" I shout.

I did not put everything I've built on the line for it to end like this. For her to end up with *them.*

She is *mine.*

Standing, I grab her by the hair and yank, no longer trying to be gentle.

My Rose...

"Draven!" She claws at my hands, but I hold her firm as I march us toward the ensuite.

Altered.

Tainted.

Ruined.

I don't release her until I've slammed the bathroom door shut behind us, sealing her into this smaller, enclosed space with me. She scrambles to distance herself from me and runs a hand through her mussed hair, attempting to relieve the sting of having strands ripped from her scalp.

The sight almost makes me chuckle.

How could she do this to me?

I'm a monster.

"Get undressed, Rose." My voice is dark, and the order makes her pale.

Her eyes dart around the room, and I smirk as she realizes that there's nowhere to hide. There's nothing she can put between us, nothing that will save her from my anger, and that realization is quick to settle over her. The defiance in her stance visibly deflates, and fear skates onto her features.

"N-no." She lifts her chin — as if acting strong will do anything other than add to the burning flame stoking in my chest — and wraps her arms around herself protectively.

The movement draws my eyes to the hoodie covering her, and I inhale sharply. "Is that one of theirs?"

My blood boils.

Disgusting, ruined...

I storm toward her, only pausing long enough to grab my straight razor from a nearby drawer.

Tainted Rose.

I flick it open as I grab the collar of the sweatshirt, my grip around it tight enough to keep her from running as she twists in my hold.

"Draven, stop!" she screams, her fists pounding against my chest.

I ignore her onslaught of punches and grit my teeth as I press the razor against the fabric. It takes effort to slice through the thickness of it, but despite her efforts, I manage to get it off. With trembling lips, she shies away from me once I tear the fabric from her body and toss it to the floor at my feet, seething.

Burn it. Burn it!

I kick it away from us, unwilling to even *look* at it any longer, before I jab a finger over her shoulder.

"Get. In," I bark the order, and she winces, looking behind her at the shower.

She starts to shake her head, and unwilling to tolerate her defiance any longer, I slap her, hard enough to make my palm sting. Her head snaps to the side, and a small squeak escapes her lips as tears well in her eyes.

"I will not have you in my house reeking of *them*," I spit, my hands rough and unkind as I grab at the straps of her tank top.

I slice them away from her shoulders, and yank the thin workout top away from her, exposing her breasts. She's whimpering, trembling as she attempts to shield herself from my view, but she doesn't understand.

I can't look at her like this.

I can't tolerate her fucking presence until they've been rinsed from her skin.

"Get in the fucking shower, Rose. Now!" I curse, forcing her backward. She's too shocked to fight me, her arms wrapped around her chest as I shove her into the stall. "I will make you clean again, Rose."

I turn on the water, and she jumps as the cold spray hits her bare back, but she doesn't move to step out of the stream.

Good. She's learning.

"Take them off, Rose." I gesture toward the leggings beginning to cling to her skin, but she doesn't move, her eyes locked on the shaving knife still clutched in my hand.

I roll my eyes and crouch, prepared to slice them off her too, but she steps back, stopping me.

"W-wait. I-I'll do it." Her voice wobbles, and my jaw tightens.

Her tears mix with the water pouring down her head and face, but they stir no sympathy in me. There's nothing left in me but anger, and the desperate need to fucking *fix* it.

She will be perfect again.

She hooks her fingers into the waistband of her pants and drags them down her pale, curvy legs. She doesn't look at me as she kicks them off, and I give her a stiff nod of approval as I pick them up to discard them. Now she's naked, the rapidly heating water will rinse off whatever trace they might have left on her skin, but still...

It's not enough.

My eyes whirl around the stall, and an idea sparks through my mind once I see the body wash on my shelf.

I will make her clean.

She *must* be made clean.

Chapter Twenty-Five

Brielle

I'm shivering despite the hot water pounding against my back and head. I'm not cold. I'm *terrified.*

"Clean. Clean." Draven is repeating the word under his breath, low enough that it's almost incomprehensible over the sound of water splashing against the tile.

He shakes his head and steps into the stall, taking up too much space. I press back, desperate to keep him from touching me, as his eyes fly around like a wild animal's.

God, please.

"You will be perfect again, Rose." He reaches out, and I flinch.

He grabs a bottle of soap from a shelf beside me, and it's as he's pouring it onto a mesh scrub cloth that I realize what he's going to do.

"No." I try to duck around him, but he grabs my wrist in a punishing hold and yanks.

I scream as he rips my arm away from my body, and writhe as he drags the soapy rag up my skin roughly, leaving a trail of pink flesh in its wake.

"Stop! Let go of me." I try to pull free, but he only tightens his hold, twisting my wrist until a loud snap echoes through the stall.

Pain spirals up my arm, and I scream again as white pain blinds me.

Oh my god.

My wrist.

My wrist.

"Stop fucking fighting me!" he booms over the sound of my cries, and I shake my head, thrashing.

It hurts.

It hurts so fucking bad.

He curses and shoves me back against the wall. Releasing my wrist, he shoves his forearm across my chest, pinning me in place. I breathe out a hissed cry at the relief, but the feeling is quickly washed away as he presses the razor blade against my throat.

"Stop this, Rose. Stop. This is for your own fucking good, do you understand me?" he shouts.

The sharp edge cuts into my skin, not deep enough to do any true damage, but deep enough to make his point clear.

No more fighting.

I nod my understanding, and gingerly clutch my wrist to my stomach as he removes his arm from my chest. Keeping the blade to my throat, he continues his assault. It's uncomfortable, especially when a freshly scrubbed section is hit by the scalding water pouring from the showerhead, but nothing compares to the stabbing pain in my wrist. My fingers are tingling, and despite my effort, I can't get them to move without nearly doubling over from the pain.

It's broken.

He broke my wrist.

Fuck.

"Do not move," he growls, and the razor presses harder into my flesh.

My entire body goes rigid as he begins scrubbing my lower stomach, and I whimper.

"P-please," I whisper, but whatever part of him might have been merciful toward me broke when I admitted my love for the Grimm Brothers. He forces his hand between my legs, and I shake, uncaring of the blade that's cutting into my skin. "Draven, please!"

He ignores my cries and scrubs at me harshly, fighting my legs as I try desperately to close them. It's violating, humiliating, and bile burns the back of my throat.

I'm going to be sick.

Blood trickles down my neck from the shallow wound he's created, but if he notices, he doesn't care.

He straightens once he's happy with his work, and drops the rag to the ground at our feet. "Turn around."

I move, my entire body stiff as I spin to face the wall. I feel broken, so fucking *broken*.

"Do not move." The repeated order fills the stall as he begins fumbling around behind me, the sound of his zipper making my blood run cold.

I'm transported back to the clearing, to the men that tried to assault me, and a sob wracks through my chest.

"P-please, d-don't." I shake my head, but with a broken wrist, and no weapon, I'm not sure how I'm going to get out of this.

He doesn't respond, and I stiffen as he grabs my shoulder.

Fight, Brielle.

Survive.

I turn, prepared to fight with whatever strength I can muster, but when I see the jerking motion of his arm, I whip back around.

He's masturbating.

I try not to gag, my throat tight with disgust as I pull in a sharp breath through my gritted teeth. The sound of his hand sliding against his own skin fills the suddenly too tight space, but I don't move, afraid that drawing attention to myself might entice him to violate me further. His hand moves from my shoulder, stroking my wet hair, and he groans, getting closer to the edge.

I stand as still as I can, but as his release spills over my ass, I can no longer fight the bile burning my throat.

I vomit.

"Fuck, Rose," Draven yells, and scrambles from the shower.

He waits until I've finished retching, until my stomach is empty of what little contents it had held, to turn off the shower. Shaking, I slip to the floor, no longer able to hold myself up. My teeth chatter, my body cold, despite the heat radiating off my raw pink skin.

"Get up." I don't know when Draven left the room, but as I slowly rise to my feet, I notice that he's changed into dry clothes. He wraps a towel around my shoulders, and grabs my elbow, steadying me as I step from the stall. "Good girl."

I wince at his praise, hating the sound of those familiar words coming from him.

"Get dressed." He holds out a white T-shirt, and I snatch it from him with my good hand, desperate to cover my body.

I try to dry myself, but with him watching me and my wrist screaming in protest, I quickly drop the towel and tug the shirt over my head. It barely covers my ass, and without underwear, I'm left feeling more exposed than I had in the shower with his cum on my skin.

A knock on the bathroom door makes me jump, and Draven crosses toward it, muttering.

He opens the door, and someone I can't see begins to speak. "Sir? It's time. What are your orders?"

It's time?

Time for what?

Draven hisses something before he turns back to me and motions me forward. I don't move, and he growls.

"You're going to learn to listen to me, Rose. Now, come." He snaps his hand out and latches onto my bad wrist, uncaring as I begin screaming and crying. "You'll learn to love me, too, but first, we need to rectify your little *predicament*."

Chapter Twenty-Six

Xander

My fingers are numb from the tight grip I have on the steering wheel. I'm driving recklessly, and while that realization would normally deter me, it's no longer a sufficient enough threat to pull my foot off the gas.

Fuck living, if I have to do it without her.

"How much further?" I question.

"Five minutes," Everett growls.

He's sitting in the passenger seat beside me, checking the assault rifle in his lap. Rhys is in the backseat, flicking his thumb over the spark wheel of his lighter. Repeatedly.

"Quit fucking around with that damn thing and focus, Blaze!" I shout.

He grunts, in acknowledgment or in irritation, I can't be sure, not without eyeing him in the rearview, and I refuse to take my eyes off the road no matter how sparse the population on this side of the city. He knows my anger isn't directed at him.

There are a few mansions scattered every hundred acres or so, each lavish lot of land surrounded by a reinforced iron fence. If Draven Augustin's property has the same boarder, it's going to make our entrance a little more... *noticeable.*

"It's the next one," Everett confirms and straightens in his seat.

I roll my neck, attempting to ease the tension rooted in my shoulders, a feeling I'd almost forgotten since Brielle entered my home.

We are getting her back.

My eyes scan the driveway, the gate coming up ahead and, finally, I risk a glance at my brothers.

"Brace yourselves."

I press the pedal into the floor, forcing the SUV to an even higher speed.

Then, I ram the fucking gate.

* * * *

Draven

They're so goddamned predictable.

"Alert the others, and stick to the plan. I want them dead." My voice is darker than I've ever heard it, my eyes locked on the smoking vehicle displayed on my monitors.

"Yes, sir." Conrad, the man I'd planted within the prison to intervene in George's fate there, stands from his seat.

He'd been useful in ensuring Rose's father was placed in solitary, and became even more indispensable when the man seized and required hospitalization. He knew how to get in contact with Joe, the head of the Grimm Brother's security team. It all fell into place so perfectly, I was able to bring my Rose home.

I watch as the man grabs his gun off the desk, but he pauses on the way out of the security room, his eyes traveling to Rose. She's hovering where I left her, with her broken wrist clutched uselessly to her chest. My T-shirt does little to cover her, and with her wet hair, the fabric has turned almost sheer, revealing her ample cleavage and curves.

Fuck.

I clear my throat, irritated, and Conrad jumps, quickly retreating from the security room.

He's lucky I need him.

Pacing, I eye the monitors again, scanning my ruined front gate and the car those fuckers have yet to exit. Maybe if I'm lucky, they saved me the trouble.

"Please, Draven, just let me go," Rose whispers, and I growl, turning on her.

She's disheveled, her eyes swollen and puffy from crying, and her neck is covered in dried blood. She's watching the monitors, her chest unmoving as she waits, shifting on her feet. Her lips move, as if she's muttering something then she sighs as the driver's side door opens.

Fuck.

"We're ending this, Rose. Once they're out of the way, you'll learn to love me," I growl.

And if that doesn't work, well...I guess it's a good thing I always have a backup plan.

* * * *

Rhys

My ears are ringing.

Particles of dust, having escaped with the explosion of airbags, float freely around the cabin as we slip from the mangled vehicle. Sure, it wasn't the most practical way to get in but now one side of the gate is hanging lopsided enough for our bodies to squeeze through.

"That's one way to make a fucking entrance," Everett grumbles, rubbing small circles against his temple.

That probably hurt worse with a concussion.

We're ducked behind the open passenger door, using it as cover in anticipation of a thunderstorm of gunfire that's not yet begun.

"Brass. Blaze," Xander calls through the car. "Stay tight on my flanks and keep your head low. We go on my count."

I peer around the door, following the perfectly manicured path up to the front door. There's no alarm going off. No shouting from distant men warning us to leave, or *else*. There's not even a fluttering of curtains to bode an onlooker that's just disappeared in a hurry.

What if they aren't here?

No.

I won't let myself think like that.

She's here, and we're getting her *back*.

On Xander's count, we rush forward, guns raised and ready. We came prepared for a fight, so we aren't surprised when the front door opens and a few men file out with their own weapons drawn. Xander and Everett shoot in tandem, their reaction times trained to near perfection. The bullets tear into the first two men before they've had a chance to fire, leaving me to handle the third.

I shoot as he pulls his trigger.

A bullet whizzes past my head as mine strikes its target.

Fucker.

Everett makes quick work of the other two men who have slipped outside, and before I know it, we're tucking ourselves to either side of the opening.

The storm we'd been expecting begins. Bullets are popping off in rapid succession, striking the walls and door with enough force to send pieces flying off.

Xander manages a peek inside and curses. "The fucker's playing all his cards."

"How many?" I question.

"Not enough to keep her from us," Everett growls.

"We need to get in and get out. I don't want her inside of this house for one second longer than necessary," Xander barks over the noise, his eyes raking over each of us as we nod. "Good. We'll split up like we planned."

He fires his rifle four times, a quick burst of bullets, before rushing inside.

Everett looks across the opening to me, raising a brow.

"Go. I'll cover you," I call.

I watch as he disappears, and shoot down an attacker that's appeared around the side of the house. Once I'm sure there are no others approaching from outside, I pull in a sharp breath, and lunge through the front door.

We're coming, Flower.

Chapter Twenty-Seven

Brielle

Despite the thick walls of the security room Draven has forced me into, I can still hear the hail of bullets tearing through the house above us. I'm staring at the screens, hoping to catch another glimpse of them.

Of my men.

My eyes flick from one monitor to the next, and I frown when my gaze catches on a black screen. It's been turned off, and while I'm sure Draven would like me to believe that it's simply not functioning properly, I know better.

He's hiding something.

An escape route?

More men readying themselves to attack?

Or something worse?

My mind drifts to the basement back at the Grimm Brothers' home, and I can't help the terror that twists my stomach. He's been preparing for *six* years to bring me here and make me fall in love with him. After the incident in the shower, there's no doubt in my mind that he's willing to use force to do so.

What kind of torture is he hiding with that black screen?

I shiver and retreat as he crosses toward me, sweat beading along his brow. The gun he'd used in the hospital is back in his grasp, and he points it at me as he grabs my elbow, tugging me toward the desk.

"Sit," he orders, grabbing my shoulder and shoving me down into the office chair.

I grit my teeth and try to ignore the pain being jostled causes in my arm, and squeak as he spins the chair so I'm no longer facing the monitors.

"Stay," he barks, and again, I feel like I'm nothing more than a dog to him.

One that he expects to obey his commands.

Pressing my lips together, I pull in a steadying breath and stand. Forcing my shoulders back, I turn to face him, determined to appear strong despite the tremor in my legs.

"You owe me an explanation, Draven." I lift my chin and do my best to keep my voice even. "I want answers."

He looks exasperated as his eyes jump from me to the monitors and back again. I use the distraction to eye them myself, and when I spot Xander take down one of Draven's men, I have to keep myself from bouncing up and down with joy.

"What answers?" he demands.

"I want to know why you killed Lincoln." I'm stalling him, attempting to distract him long enough that I can bolt for the door.

If I can get it open, and find my men, we can escape before anyone else gets hurt.

"Jesus, Rose, now?" He rolls his eyes and waves his arms. "Isn't it obvious? Once he knew who I was, he started extorting me for money. It was the only way to keep him from airing my dirty laundry."

I walk around the desk, watching as he turns to scan the monitors again. Now that I know who he is, I understand why any information tied to my social security number was disappearing. Of course someone with his skill set would be able to erase it or store it out of sight, and while I may not truly understand the reasoning, I can guess it has something to do with his desperation to control me. Sure.

But why Sammy's?

"You used men tied to the Wolves to throw the Grimm Brothers off," I state, and when he nods, his eyes jumping to me, I continue, "But why get them involved in the first place? Why frame my father?"

He drops his head back. "With him out of the picture, you'd have no one to care for you. I thought it'd be easier to convince you to come home with me."

"You wanted them to kill my father," I murmur.

"They were never supposed to take you." For the first time, I can hear the remorse in his tone. "I never would have arranged for those monsters to take you."

Monsters?

I laugh. "They are not monsters, Draven, you are."

My words wound him. The air rushes from his lungs, and he takes an unsteady step back, frowning.

Now, Brielle.

I turn and race for the door. I can hear him yelling, cursing me, rushing after me, but I don't stop. Yanking the door aside slows me down, the heavy metal hard to maneuver with one arm, and he catches me as I'm crossing into the basement, his hand snagging my shirt.

He rips me back, and I scream loud enough to make my ears ring. "Help, I'm here!"

He clamps a hand over my mouth and pulls me toward the security room. I kick, trying desperately to land a blow, and screech as he tosses me to the ground.

"Enough!" he shouts.

His foot crashes into my side, hard enough to knock the air from my lungs, and I gasp, unable to breathe. I twist, trying to shield myself as another kick strikes my leg, and then my injured wrist.

My scream makes him jump, my throat raw as the sound rips through the basement. He glances over his shoulder, and curses again, before smashing his foot against my head, silencing me.

Please, please…

I'm helpless against the darkness that devours me.

Chapter Twenty-Eight

Everett

Safely hidden inside behind pillars, Xander and Rhys draw the attention—and gunfire—while I study the foyer. David had sent over an original floor plan, but there was no way of knowing if changes were made during—or since—construction until we got inside.

There are three halls leading off the main foyer, one closed door, and a massive split staircase that leads to a second and third story. So far, it all appears to be identical to the blueprints we've seen, so I signal to my brothers, letting them know we're good to stick to the plan. Rhys and I are going to take the upper levels while Xander stays on the main. Whoever finds Brielle first is supposed to contact the others, but *only* after she's safe.

"Got it!" Rhys calls, spotting my signal, and Xander grunts his confirmation.

With my brothers fully informed, I poke my head back around the pillar and fire, taking out a man who'd been inching toward Rhys. We can't tell how many men we're up against in a house this size, and if that weren't disadvantage enough, I can see that a few of the fuckers are wearing body armor.

"Goddamnit," I curse, and growl as a bullet launches itself into the pillar by my thigh.

I start picking off a few of the outliers that hover near the edge of the room, and once they're out of the way, it looks like we're only left to contend with the handful remaining on the ground floor.

"I'm pushing forward," Rhys calls over the chaos.

"Not yet, Blaze!" Xander barks.

Rhys grits his teeth but remains planted. Two men inch forward, and the wall behind me explodes as bullets whizz past me and lodge into the drywall. Xander takes them out, and in the brief pause of commotion as they crash to the ground, I hear it.

Screaming.

"Brielle." Panic and guilt lance through me, and suddenly, I'm rushing forward without thinking.

"Brass! Stop!" Xander shouts, but it's too late.

I can't get her fear-stricken face out of my head, an image of her that's been firmly planted in my mind since I realized that she'd had to face Draven, without me.

"Brass!" Rhys calls.

I move toward the stairs, too preoccupied with firing at a man hiding on the second floor, to respond.

I should have looked up.

Rhys

Brass storms forward, his gun raised as he shoots a man hiding on the second story. He doesn't notice the guy emerging from the side room to his left, and I curse, rushing forward.

"Brass!" I shout, taking aim and pulling the trigger. My gun clicks, but nothing fires from the barrel. It's jammed. *Fuck.* "Brass!"

He doesn't look away from the new man he's taken aim at. He's too lost in his head to hear me.

Xander, having heard the commotion, has turned, his weapon trained on the man threatening our brother. He shoots, but despite the bullet he rockets into the man's stomach, a bullet still fires off at Everett.

I shout and throw myself forward, tackling my brother with enough force to send us both crashing to the floor as the bullet audibly whizzes past. Pain tears through my temple as we fall, and my teeth gnash together as a realization tears through me.

The fucker hit me.

"Blaze! Rhys. Fuck." Everett is kneeling over me, his hand suddenly pressed against the side of my head. *How the hell…* "What the hell were you thinking?"

I'm alive?

"God, fucking hell, Rhys."

I push at his hands, my head swimming with adrenaline, and lift my fingers to inspect the damage myself. A long gash has been torn from the back of my head, through my ear, and across my temple, marking the bullet's path.

It's just a scratch.

"I told you I'd cover you." I choke out a strangled laugh, the entire ordeal making me woozy.

"Blaze!" Xander is clearing the room, his head on a swivel as he checks to make sure there are no further threats.

"I'm good." I force myself up.

The room spins a little, and blood is dripping a sticky trail down my face, but I'm alive.

Everett wouldn't have been so lucky.

"You need to get out of here," Xander calls to me over his shoulder.

He's moved off toward one hall and is reloading his rifle, his eyes bouncing from one dead body to the next.

"No. We're sticking to the plan." I shake my head and take Everett's outstretched hand, allowing him to help me to my feet.

I grab my weapon from the ground and start working to clear the jam as Everett tears off the sleeve of his shirt. I'm not sure what he's doing until he starts dressing my wound.

"Thank you, Rhys," he murmurs once he's finished.

I nod and clap his shoulder before we begin reloading our weapons. It's not something he needs to be grateful for. I'd do anything for our family.

If that means dying to protect them, so be it.

"Let's go find our girl."

Everett

Rhys and I watch as Xander starts down a side hall, hoping and praying that, one way or another, we find Brielle soon.

"Come on." Rhys, now patched to the best of my ability, starts climbing the stairs, his gun aimed and ready.

I'm still a little dazed, but I do my best to shake it off, thoroughly scanning each body I step over to ensure they're dead.

I don't want any more surprises.

"Are you good to take this floor?" I ask Rhys as we reach second floor landing.

He nods and silently shifts forward, his hand skimming the wall before he glances around the corner. There must not be anyone waiting on the other side, because he disappears around it without another word, determined to find Brielle.

Nodding, I lift my gun and climb the rest of the stairs, thankful that when I reach the third floor, it's devoid of any other threat.

For now.

Stalking forward, I peer around the corner, and once I've determined it's safe, I round it. I start clearing rooms. I don't leave a single door unchecked, worried that if I miss one closet, one bathroom, one fucking laundry room, I might be missing Brielle.

When I make it to the final corner, the sound of someone muttering catches my attention, and I pause, pressing against the wall. They're too far off for me to make out what they're saying, but the fear and the anger in their voice carries down the hall.

I peer around the corner, my rifle clutched to my side. I curse when I spot a solitary guard pacing in front of the last door in the hall, and groan when I realize that I *recognize* the fucker.

Conrad.

His weapon hangs loosely in his grip, and he shakes his head as he continues muttering under his breath. I'm sure he heard the fight downstairs. I'm sure that he knows the other men Draven hired to fight us are dead. So, why is he still waiting here? What could Draven possibly be paying him to wait on death's door? Why doesn't he run?

I shake my head, pushing away the questions. None of it matters. The *only* thing that matters is that he's standing between me and Brielle.

I don't think twice before I shoot the unsuspecting man. I don't feel guilty as I kick his dead body for good measure. My heart thumps unsteadily as I step over him and push open the unlocked door.

I quickly scan the spacious bedroom, but it's not Brielle that I find cowering beside the bed.

Is this…?

"Samuel?"

A boy is curled into a tight ball on the floor by the bed, his hands pressed tightly over his ears. He doesn't make any move to respond, his watery eyes searching me and the weapon in my hand with fear.

He's scared.

He's scared of me.

"Are you Sammy?" I adjust the strap on my rifle and tuck it behind me out of sight. Holding my hands up, I inch into the room, slow enough that he can anticipate my movements. "My name is Everett. I'm a friend of Brielle's. Of Bri's."

I use the nickname she'd called herself in the hospital with her father, and at the sound of it, his shoulders relax slightly. He lowers his hands, and nods hesitantly, confirming my earlier question.

Sammy.

What the fuck is he doing here?

"The bad guys call her Rose," he murmurs, lifting his eyes—the color identical to his sisters—to meet mine. "Mr. Augustin said I'd have to call her that, too. Once we started acting like a family."

The fucker.

"It's okay, Sammy. I'm going to get you out of here, all right?" I kneel in front of him and glance over my shoulder toward the door.

There's so much danger, gore and *death* beyond that threshold. How the fuck am I going to get him out of here unscathed? Physically and mentally?

Thinking on my feet, I reach up and tear a strip off a nearby pillowcase then hold it up to him. "I'm going to cover your eyes, okay?"

He shies away from me, skeptical.

"I saw you take Bri..." he whispers, his lips trembling. *He was there...* "D-do you promise you're a good guy?"

He's watching me with a mixture of fear and hope that cracks my chest open. How can I ruin that with the truth? I've *never* been a good guy, but right now, I'm willing to do anything, or be anyone, that this kid needs me to be.

A good guy.

"I promise, Sammy."

Chapter Twenty-Nine

Xander

I've cleared almost the entire first floor, and still *nothing.* I curse inwardly as I yank open another door.
Closet.

I duck behind the door and check my cell. There's no message from either of my brothers confirming that they've found her and are out, so I continue on, pulling on another handle.
Bathroom.

I glance around the space and eye each open door with a scowl. So far, the floorplan has been identical to the one David was able to scrounge up, so that means...

I press my ear against the wood of the next door over and listen. I don't hear anything coming from the other side, no hushed voices or cocking guns, so I pull it open, smirking.
The basement.

There haven't been any more idiots with guns posted on this floor, so either he sent them all to cover the front of the house, or he split them. Some to protect the entrance. The rest? I expect them to be with him, protecting him and ensuring Brielle is kept from us, but as I peer around the wall shielding the stairs from the rest of the room, I'm surprised to find no guns trained in my direction.

"We've been waiting for you, Beast."

As I peer back around the wall, I see him. Draven Augustin is crouched just beyond an open steel door, a gun in his hand, a smirk on his face. He's hovering over Brielle, who lies on the ground, unmoving.

The sight makes me growl, and I rush forward without thinking. I don't clear the rest of the room. I can't focus on any other possible threat. Not when one is pointed at our half-naked woman's head.

"Ah, ah." He clicks his tongue, and winds his hands through her hair, yanking her limp head off the ground. A small whimper comes from the back of her throat, and her eyes flutter, although I'm not sure she's truly conscious as he presses the barrel against her temple. "Don't do anything stupid, Beast."

"Let her go." My voice shakes with fury as I reluctantly take in her broken and exposed body.

I'm going to fucking kill him.

I can see a few injuries from here, but can't pull my gaze away from her wet hair, or the water that's soaked through her shirt.

He made her shower.

Has he touched her?

Raped her?

I clutch my gun so tightly that my hands shake, and he laughs, noticing.

"You're in no position to be making demands, Beast. I have something you want, so you'll be listening to me." He yanks her head back, stirring another cry from her. "Drop your weapon."

"N-no," Brielle's broken voice fills the room, and it draws me forward, desperate.

"Drop your weapon!" he repeats.

He straightens slightly, and the movement pulls Brielle up. She's still too far gone to hold herself up, no doubt suffering from a head injury, so her body hangs limply from the grip he has on her wet waves. The new angle twists her body awkwardly, and again, she cries out.

"All right, all right. Fuck," I curse, unable to stand the pain that's warped her features.

I drop to one knee and set my gun on the floor, my eyes locked on him as I wait for his next demand.

"Slide it here." He presses the silencer harder into her temple.

She whimpers, my nickname falling broken from her lips, "B-east."

I'm not sure if it's a plea for me to listen, or fight, but I cave to the unpredictable man holding the gun to her head.

The metal of my gun scratches against the ground as it slides forward, but the noise is quickly drowned out by his laughter. He releases her, and she falls back against the ground, a sick thump echoing through the room as her head strikes the floor. It makes my stomach churn and my jaw tighten with anger as he steps over her limp body.

I wait for him to raise his gun. I grit my teeth in preparation of a bullet hurling in my direction, but as I lift my gaze, I see his attention is no longer on me. He's staring at the gun I've just slid toward him, his shoulders drooping as he stoops forward to reach for it.

Big mistake, Draven.

I take the opportunity his distraction has provided, and lunge, tackling him. I hear Brielle's labored breathing as I twist the gun out of his hand, snapping a few of his fingers in the process. I can almost *smell* the blood leaking from her skull as I drive my fist into his face.

"You will *never* touch her again." I'm straddling him, one hand wrapped around his shirt as the other lifts, prepared to deliver another blow. "Do you fucking hear me? Never again."

He screams, and rips wildly at my clothes, my hair, anything he can use to try to cause pain. Too bad for him, my anger has blinded me. He thrashes and reaches for his gun as I strike him again, breaking his nose. I hold him close to my face, and chuckle darkly as he writhes, trying to get away from me.

"You wanted the Beast? Well, you've fucking got him. I'm going to enjoy killing you."

This fucker has been stalking Brielle for years. He's ruined her family. Stolen her sense of home. Security. *Love.*

Pictures of her are plastered all over the walls of this house, and I shout, raging.

"She is *ours*." I spit the words and drive my fist down into his face again.

I'm too enraged to notice the blade he pulls from his pocket until I feel the metal of it biting into my flesh, but still, it's not enough to dull my fury. He's slashing at me desperately.

"I'm going to take my time with you, Draven. You're going to regret the day that you laid eyes on what's ours. Do you fucking hear me?"

The sound of whimpering breaks through the sheen of anger that's blinded me. *Amour.* Is she in pain? Or is she scared...of *me?*

Of the Beast that's awoken.

I'm only distracted for a second, but it's long enough. Draven drives his blade between my ribs. Pain explodes like a bomb has just detonated in my chest, and I choke. I can't get in any air.

Fuck.

I fall off him, my hands clutched to my side as I gasp like a fish out of water. I'm suffocating.

It fucking *hurts.*

Fuck!

He stands over me, laughing. Or, at least I think he's laughing. I can't hear anything over the sound of my own choking.

He boots me in the side.

I don't feel it. My body is shaking. Going into shock. Am I dying? After all I've survived...is this really it for me?

Pulling in a shallow breath, I turn to look for Brielle. If this is the end, the last thing I want to see is her.

She's standing.

The one thing...

She's holding Draven's gun.

I did right...

Her arm is raised, shaking, as she aims like we showed her.

Was loving you, Brielle Beaumont.

She fires.

I love you.

Then everything goes dark.

Chapter Thirty

Brielle

Before meeting the Grimm Brothers, I'd never contemplated what it might be like to take someone's life. As a nurse, I'd sworn to save as many as I could. But after uncovering the darker side of the world, of *my* world, I understand that in the end, there may not be another choice. I remember thinking that if—and when—the time came, it would be difficult for me to make that decision.

To kill someone.

But lying there, struggling to remain conscious, watching as Draven drives his blade into Xander's side, I'm surprised by the awareness that settles over me.

I know what I have to do.

Draven's gun is lying on the ground beside me. It's warm in my hands, and again, heavier than I anticipate it being. My head reels as I stand, and my arm shakes with the effort of holding it aloft with one hand.

I aim for Draven's center mass.

And fire.

The noise that erupts through the room as the bullet rocks from the barrel is deafening. The gun kicks in my hand, but I hit my target.

Draven falls.

I stagger toward Xander.

"Beast? Beast!" I'm shouting. It sounds muffled to my ringing ears, but my throat is raw as I kneel beside him. "Xander. Xander, look at me."

He doesn't move. His shallow breathing sputters past his parted lips.

"I'm sorry. I'm so sorry." I'm shaking, my adrenaline fading.

The pounding in my skull is returning. Draining me. Pulling me toward the darkness again.

I touch his cheek.

Kiss his lips.

I lay my head on his chest, letting the unsteady rise and fall of it lure me down, down, down…

I close my eyes and cling to him.

It's over.

It's finally over, and I'm so fucking *tired*.

"I love you, Beast."

* * * *

Everything is spinning as I drift somewhere between consciousness and nothingness. My thoughts are scattered, and despite my best efforts, they slip through my fingers like sand when I try to grasp them.

Where am I?

What happened?

I keep pulling for memories, but the only ones floating within reach seem more like a horrible nightmare than reality.

Did I really kill Draven?

Or am I still lying on the ground of that security room, bruised, humiliated and *terrified?*

The world shifts, becoming sharp—too sharp—as the pain builds until it's nearly unbearable, before it blurs and turns numb again. My eyes don't want to open, and my body feels heavy, like it's sinking. I want to give in to the darkness, where there's no pain, but just as I begin walking that edge, something tugs on my awareness, and I'm dragged back.

I don't know how long I float like that. In and out, like an ocean tide being manipulated by the moon. Voices come and go, but they're too distant to understand, too muffled to be comprehensible. I try to speak, desperate to ask for help, but it feels like a rock is lodged in my throat, keeping me silent.

Something squeezes my hand. The feeling filters through the haze, and I cling to it, desperate to fight my way back to the surface.

Come on, Brielle.

Fight.

I try to move my limbs, but they feel like they're weighed down by lead and they don't budge.

Try something else, something smaller.

My eyes twitch, fluttering open a smidge, but it's bright—*too bright*—and I can't see.

Ugh, god, please.

I open my mouth, but my throat is dry and raw. I can't form words, just a rasping, gravely cry that frustrates me to no end.

"Brielle?" A voice snakes through the pounding in my head, and again, I try to open my eyes.

This time, shapes come into focus, and eventually, those shapes morph into faces.

Faces I recognize.

My men.

Well...

Two of them.

Chapter Thirty-One

Rhys

"How horrible. Can you imagine burning to death?"

Two nurses are gossiping, their hushed whispers rising to greet me as I walk down the hall, flowers in hand.

"No." The older of the two shivers. "What a slow and painful way to go."

If only his death had been so 'horrific'.

"It's such a shame. A man that attractive and rich?" The younger one sighs, and I roll my eyes before ducking into the room.

Everett is sitting in a chair beside Brielle's bed, asleep, his head dropped back against the wall behind him. We've been switching out, rotating between her room and Xander's, for the past two days, and the lack of sleep is beginning to catch up with us.

I set the vase of flowers on a nearby table and round the bed, stroking a hand along her warm cheek.

"I'm back, Flower," I murmur, my eyes scouring her pale and bruised face.

Oh, Brielle...

She has two fractures, one in her wrist that had to be set and cast, and another along the front of her skull. The doctor who'd originally evaluated her upon our arrival stated that it and her concussion were likely caused by blunt force trauma. Of course, he didn't need to elaborate. It doesn't take a wild fucking imagination to figure out what happened. The fucker *kicked* her, hard enough to cause a break in her skull.

I grit my teeth and drop my gaze, my stomach roiling as I remember the next words that'd come out of that man's mouth.

"I want to perform a rape kit."

He'd been unnecessarily insistent, but thankfully, Dr. Patel — the physician we keep on our payroll — had just received the needed clearances to provide care with the hospital, and he swooped into action. He knew from the look Everett and I exchanged, not to continue pushing *that* examination. We refused to cause more trauma, especially while she was unconscious and unable to consent. There was no point, anyway. We fucker who'd hurt her was dead, and there was no greater punishment than that. So instead, he re-evaluated her head injury, and ensured we had all the needed information for her recovery. He's told us, again and again, that the bruising to her brain isn't severe enough to cause concern, but...

She still hasn't woken up, yet.

"I'm sorry, Flower," I whisper and take her hand — the one *not* wrapped in hardened plaster — in mine.

Does she know we're here?

Just wake up, Brielle. Please. Please.

"How's Xander?" Everett, who's roused himself from his fitful and unsatisfying sleep, sits forward in his chair, stretching.

I tug my gaze away from Brielle for a moment, before resuming my scan of her fragile frame. I've counted each visible injury a dozen times. I wish knowing the bastard is dead would do something to soothe the burning hate in my heart.

"Dr. Patel removed his chest tube this morning. He's hoping that the pneumothorax will heal on its own, without surgery, but—" I sigh, my teeth grinding together. "They're monitoring it."

"His oxygen saturation?" he questions through a yawn.

The questions have become so practiced, so frequently asked, that we don't even seem to hear the answers anymore. Unless it's something new, something *good*, we just nod and keep pushing on.

"It was still hovering around ninety-six percent when I left. He'll have the cannula until the hole closes," I reply.

Everett nods—as expected—and runs a hand along the back of his neck, his lips pressing into a thin line. He looks as exhausted as I feel, but the redness rimming his eyelids is proof enough of the pain that he must be feeling. He's refused to get any proper rest, or pain medication, which is the exact opposite of what he needs to do to treat his concussion. It's going to drag out the recovery process if he doesn't take care of it soon. I eye him now, wondering what it's going to take.

"Dr. Patel cleaned up my head." I gesture to the graze across my skull from the bullet before I motion toward him, silently inferring that he do something about his.

He just rolls his eyes. "It's just a concussion."

"Sure, but it'd be good to get his opinion. He could at least give you something to help you sleep." I shrug.

He waves off my concern and stands, stretching.

"Do you want a coffee? I'm going to step out and update Mrs. Claebourne—"

A garbled cry interrupts him.

My heart leaps into my throat as Brielle's eyes flutter, her hand twitching in mine. "Brielle…?"

Her eyes open, her gaze unfocused as she scans us, and I hiss out a sigh of relief. "Oh, thank fucking god."

"We're here, Brielle." Everett strokes her cheek as she blinks, trying to clear her vision.

She frowns, her eyes jumping wildly around the room as the heart monitor attached to her begins beeping rapidly.

"You're safe, Flower. It's okay." I lean forward, stroking her hand, but she shakes her head.

"X-Xander, where—" Her voice cracks, and she winces, unable to disguise her pain. "Where i-is-"

"Shh. He's okay, pet. He's here," Everett shushes her, and I turn, grabbing a cup of water from the nearby table.

"He's in a room down the hall," I explain, and hold the straw up to her dry lips. "Here, Flower. Drink this, please."

She eyes me warily and I can't say that I blame her for her skepticism. The last she'd seen of our brother, he was bleeding out beneath her. It's understandable that she'd be uneasy accepting our reassurance about his condition when she hasn't seen him for herself. Finally, she takes the straw between her lips and takes a few hesitant sips. When she's satisfied, she leans back, flinching as she attempts to find a comfortable position.

"I'm going to grab a nurse," Everett states, but before he can rush off, Brielle squeaks a protest.

"No, p-please. Please, stay." She reaches for him, her face washing with panic, and again, the heart monitor beeps erratically.

"It's okay, pet. It's okay." He rounds back to her bedside, his thumb stroking away a tear that's slipped down her cheek. "I'm here. We're here."

"And we're not going anywhere," I add.

She sighs and nods, a tiny smile curling up the corner of her lips. "I-I love you. I love you both."

She laughs. It's a soft, surprising sound that pulls low chuckles from Everett and me as we murmur our own proclamations of love down onto her. The sound of our joined laughter melts her onto the mattress, and for a moment, she's happy. She's happy until her eyes scan the room, and she remembers that one of us is missing.

She blows a breath out past her parted lips, and attempts to sit up.

"Flower? What're you doing?" I ask, watching as she whimpers. I try to ease her back against the bed, but she fights me. "Brielle?"

"I-I have to see him. I need to see Xander." She lets out a rushed breath, and stills in my hold, tears stinging her eyes.

"Not now, pet. Please, you need to rest," Everett murmurs, but she shakes her head.

"No, no. I can't. I-I have to see him. I have to *see* him. Please. Please." She looks between us both, desperate now. "Please."

I look to my brother, lost.

Neither of us can stand the sight of her crying. "Okay, Flower. Okay." I nod, and lower myself onto the bed beside her, gently wrapping an arm around her.

"We'll figure something out, pet." Everett looks toward the door, his mind already working to conjure up a plan.

She leans into me, sniffling, and I follow Everett's eyes to the door. She wants to see Xander, and we've always been willing to move mountains to get her what she wants, but this?

How in the hell are we going to do *this*?

She's been unconscious for three days. Three. She has IV lines, a catheter and too many monitor lines to count. Not to mention the amount of strength it will take for her to sit up in a chair, and the pain that doing so will likely cause.

She glances up at me through her lashes, and I nod my head toward the door.

"We're going to need some help."

Chapter Thirty-Two

Brielle

"I *really* would prefer that you wait for the physician," a nurse, whose name I've either forgotten, or haven't been told, mutters.

It's the third or fourth time she's voiced her disapproval, and while I appreciate her concern, I'm *this* close to telling her to shut the fuck up. She's making my men share a look. A look that says *'maybe we should rethink this'* and they change their minds, I swear to god...

"Flower, maybe we should—" Rhys starts, but I shake my head.

"I'm okay." I'm not sure if I'm saying it to Rhys, the two nurses hovering, or myself, but I swing my legs off the edge of the bed, prepared to stand.

"Hang on, pet. Let us help." Everett moves toward me, and Rhys pushes a wheelchair forward.

It takes the assistance of both nurses, and my men, to get me up, disconnected from all my monitors, and transferred into the chair. I can feel their eyes tracking and tallying every wince that slips past the mask I've forced onto my face, can see the worried glances they continue to exchange.

Please, please don't change your minds...

"All right, you're good to go love." The nurse pats my shoulder. "Watch her IV line. We don't want it to get kinked."

She tosses the last bit at Rhys and Everett, who quickly nod their understanding, watching as she adjusts the lines still attached to me. I shift, trying to tug down the hospital gown, and Rhys notices, grabbing a blanket from the bed to drape over me.

"We don't have to do this now, pet," Everett murmurs.

"Yeah, it's okay to take a little more time. He's still out of it, anyway," Rhys confirms.

"No, no, I'm fine. Please, I want to see him." I try to shake my head, but the movement makes me flinch, so I still and lean back in the chair, sighing. "Please?"

The plea stirs them. Rhys takes charge of the IV pole, and Everett grabs the wheelchair, maneuvering me into the hall. It's bright, loud, and bustling with people. Doctors and nurses move throughout the space, and patients walk by, accompanied by staff, or walking with their families.

It makes my heart lurch, and I glance back toward Everett as much as the pain will allow. "Everett? My dad..."

"There's not been any change, pet." His voice is soft as he delivers the news, but honestly, I'm not sure that I was expecting anything different.

We work our way down the hall, and as we pass a waiting room, my eyes catch on the news flashing on the television screen. It's showing a fire, a *huge* fire, and as I look closer, I realize that I recognize the house.

Or what remains of it.

I open my mouth, but before I can speak, Rhys is talking, having followed my gaze. "Not here, Flower."

I'm still struggling to put together the broken pieces of what happened, but I silence the questions that build on my tongue.

Not here.

I drop my gaze, unwilling to see any other *reminders* as we continue down the hallway. It's quiet, despite the number of people lingering in the halls. *Hospital quiet.* A silence that promotes healing or some bullshit along those lines. It's something I might have believed in at one point a long time ago, before my mother spent countless *quiet* hours inside a cancer ward, or before I did my rounds in nursing school.

Quiet doesn't change anything.

Everett turns, easily steering me into a room, and it's then that I see him, Xander, my Beast, lying unconscious in a too small hospital bed. His black curls are spilling out around his head, and his large, tattooed body looks out of place against the stark white of the sheets. It's startling, seeing him so still, and *broken.* There's a nasal cannula hooked around his ears, supplying him with oxygen, and there's a million tubes and wires striking out from beneath his gown, but…he's here.

He's alive.

"Hi, Beast."

My voice catches in my throat, and tears sting my eyes as I reach for him, desperate to touch him. I trace his tattoos, and the scars that litter his skin but I'm careful not to touch his IV site.

Oh, Beast.

I'm silent as Everett and Rhys update me on his condition. On the hole torn through his lung, and the surgery that might be needed if it doesn't close on its own. Memories come back to me in disjointed snippets as if I'm watching them through mirrored, broken glass, and I wince as they continue speaking. I'd been so out of it from the beating, I'd been absolutely useless at doing something *other* than being a hostage. A distraction that got Xander stabbed and nearly fucking killed.

All of this is my fault.

My fault.

My fault.

My fault.

"I'm sorry. I'm so sorry, Xander," I whisper, guilt weighing heavily on my shoulders.

Rhys steps forward, and strokes a hand down my back before kneeling beside me. "Flower, Dr. Patel is really happy with the progress he's making."

"He's in here because of *me*." I spit the words, and flinch as I involuntarily fist my broken hand, causing pain to spiral up my arm. "I did this."

"No, pet. This isn't your fault." Everett shakes his head, and Rhys nods his agreement, squeezing my knee.

"Brielle, the only one to blame for any of this is Draven," Rhys tries, but I bite my lip, trembling.

"If I hadn't—"

"D-Don't."

Everyone jumps at the sudden interruption, and I gasp as Xander's eyes crack open a smidge. His blue orbs lock on me, and he pants as he struggles to catch his breath, but he continues anyway.

"Don't you dare fucking blame yourself for this." He has to pause to take a breath between each word, but eventually, he gets the broken sentence out.

Tears spill down my face, and I shift in my chair, desperate to close the distance between us as he shifts on the bed, attempting to sit up.

"Hang on." Rhys presses a button on the bed rail, and the hospital bed him into a better position. "Don't strain yourself."

"I'm fine." Xander grits through his teeth, and I sigh, smiling.

At least he feels okay enough to be stubborn.

"I love you, Xander." His eyes widen in surprise, and I release a small laugh at the words that have chosen now to suddenly spill past my lips. "I love you."

He's shocked, I can see it on his face, and I drop my gaze as a wave of embarrassment floods me.

He must not feel the same.

I just thought…

He grabs my chin, his arm shaking from the effort, and turns my face up so I meet his gaze.

"I. Love. You." The pause he takes between each word only emphasizes the weight behind them.

He loves me.

I lean into his touch, desperate to feel his skin against me, and somehow Everett interprets my needs. He moves, scooping me out of the wheelchair, and before I can raise a word of complaint, is settling me into the bed beside Xander.

"W-what—"

Xander shushes me, and Rhys moves to help maneuver cords out of the way. Tracking me with his eyes, Xander continues. "Stay, Amour."

"I don't want to hurt you." I try to keep my weight off him, but he shakes his head and grabs my hand.

"It's better, with you here." He coughs out with a smirk, and I eye him warily. "I-I love you —"

"Shh." It's my turn to silence him, as he leans his head back against the bed, exhausted. "Rest. We've got time."

I eye each of my men, the Grimm Brothers, who have stolen my heart. I love them. I love them all.

"So much time."

Chapter Thirty-Three

Everett

With Xander threading his fingers through her hair, Brielle is no match for the exhaustion that creeps up on her. She slumps against him, her head falling onto his shoulder, and he winces as her weight settles onto him.

"I'll move her." I step forward, prepared to lift her, but he waves me off with a growl.

"Don't you fucking dare." He scowls at me, and I hold up my hands as I lower myself back into the chair.

"How're you feeling? Dr. Patel should be making his rounds soon, but I can grab a nurse—" Rhys starts, but Xander cuts him off.

"I'm fine."

I roll my eyes and smile, glad to see that his bravado didn't take any hits during the fight.

"How bad's the damage?" Xander asks now, and I glance across the bed to Rhys, who shrugs.

"A house in embers doesn't leave much for questioning. The cops and news anchors made their own assumptions. We haven't run into any problems," Rhys explains.

Xander glances down at Brielle and, in a lowered voice, asks, "Did anyone make it out?"

"No." I scan Brielle's sleeping face and shake my head. "Draven sacrificed most of his pawns trying to keep us from getting inside. There was only one, aside from Draven, left to pick off after the initial fight."

Xander's face contorts as he tries to piece together why *one* singular fucker would have been left out of the battle, so I continue.

"I found Conrad guarding a room upstairs. Guarding Samuel."

His body tenses, and again, he looks down at Brielle.

"We haven't told her yet. He's staying with Mrs. Claebourne and her family while we're here. He seems fine physically but—" Rhys pauses and taps his temple. "It'll take some time for him to get over what he heard in that house."

Xander's jaw tenses, and he nods. "Has Brielle talked to either of you about what happened in the basement?"

His voice is raspy, and you can see the discomfort talking causes. I want to tell him to rest, but I know he won't stop until his questions are satisfied.

"No," Rhys and I reply in tandem.

"She killed h-him." His voice breaks, and he coughs, his entire body stiff with pain. With watering eyes, he looks between us as he forces back the discomfort. "She killed him to save me."

We're all silent for a moment, and I take the chance to, once again, study Brielle. I cannot fathom the strength it took for her to stand and fire a weapon, one handed, suffering from her injuries. I cannot fathom how a woman so scarred by death could make the decision to kill a man. Yet somehow, someway, our woman still managed to fire off a shot that killed the threat to our brother.

She's ours.

"Dr. Patel warned us that a lapse in memory wouldn't be surprising, given the severity of her head injury. It's possible she doesn't remember," Rhys mutters.

"What are we going to do when she *does*?" Xander's eyes drop, and defeat warps his features.

I lean forward and clasp his shoulder, trying my best to feign a confidence I'm sure doesn't meet my gaze. "We'll get her through it."

He sighs, and attempts to stifle a yawn, but it's impossible to disguise the exhaustion weighing down his eyelids.

"You should get some rest," Rhys murmurs, and leans back in his chair. "We'll keep an eye on things."

"You'll wake me once she's up?" He raises a brow at me now, and I nod.

"Yeah. I'll wake you," I confirm, although I'm not sure that I will.

He needs the rest.

Satisfied, he closes his eyes, and within seconds, he's drifted off again. His chest rises and falls slowly, and the beating of his heart monitor slows to a steady rhythm. I eye Rhys as he stands, stretching.

"I'm going to see if I can find some caffeine. Do you want anything?" he asks.

"Yeah, update Mrs. Claebourne for me, will you?" I glance at the clock, knowing she'll have been waiting for some time now.

"Sure." Rhys grimaces, knowing he's likely in for a scolding, and calls over his shoulder as he goes, "You owe me one."

I catch a glimpse of the burn tracked across his head from the bullet he took for me, and sigh.

"Yeah, I do."

Chapter Thirty-Four

Brielle

I'm not sure how or when I managed to drift off, but I wake at the feeling of arms wrapping around me. I whine as the heat of Xander's body against mine evaporates, and pry my eyes open, scowling.

"No...why?" I complain, but Everett is quick to shush me.

"Sorry, pet, but Dr. Patel is coming to make his rounds," he apologizes as he lowers me into the cold wheelchair.

Xander is still half asleep, his eyes cracked open enough to track Everett's movements as he adjust me and my IV line.

"C-Careful," he warns, and Everett grunts in understanding before waving him off.

"Where's Rhys?" I glance around the brightly lit room, but there's no sight of the green-eyed Grimm Brother.

"He's just out in the hall, updating Mrs. Claebourne." Everett pauses, and lowers himself in front of me so he can meet my gaze. "And Samuel."

My heart nearly leaps from my chest.

"S-Samuel? *My* Sammy?" I choke out, and Everett nods as tears well in my eyes. "He's okay?"

Everett cups my cheek, and swipes his thumb across my skin as tears slip down my face. "He's okay. He's safe. I found him while we were looking for you."

Sammy...

Draven had him?

I try to push the questions away as a knock sounds on the door, but it's nearly impossible to ignore the thoughts swirling through my head as Dr. Patel pushes into the room.

"I heard my patients were awake," he states, "and already causing trouble."

The black screen in the security room...

He was hiding Sammy from me.

But why?

"You'd better get used to it," Everett replies with a small smile in my direction.

I can't muster up the strength to return it, my mind still reeling with questions.

I was always his goal...why take Sammy?

Why?

Dr. Patel shuffles into the space, shifting around me and Everett so he can take the open place beside Xander's bed. "How're you feeling, Mr. Grimm?"

He wanted me to love him.

He was going to make me comply.

One way, or another.

I shiver at the realization as Xander mutters a small, "*Fine*," under his breath, and turn my attention to Dr.

Patel as he begins to examine him. I try my best to follow the evaluation, wanting to mentally note any place that makes Xander wince, but my head starts to pound, making it difficult to concentrate.

"I'm pleased with how this looks," Dr. Patel murmurs as he checks the site where Xander's chest tube was removed. "Any pain here?"

"No," Xander grumbles, but he still flinches under Dr. Patel's ministrations.

"And if I offered you pain meds, I'm sure you'd —"

"Decline," Xander confirms with a grunt, his eyes jumping to Rhys as he re-enters the room.

"Well, you'll be with us until that hole closes and I'm satisfied that you're oxygenating well on room air, so if you change your mind..." Dr. Patel jots something down on the chart in his hand, and waves off Xander's building complaint. "I'll order updated images at the end of the week and until then, you're on bedrest, Mr. Grimm."

I bite my lip as Xander curses, and do my best to suppress the pain that's budding through my skull as I rerun everything that Dr. Patel's told us through my head. He'd mentioned expected recovery, signs of infection, and possible surgical procedures to correct the pneumothorax if it doesn't make enough progress on its own. It's a lot to wrap my head around, on top of keeping the pain at bay.

"And you, Ms. Beaumont? How're you feeling?" Dr. Patel turns to me now, an eyebrow lifted. "Any nausea or vomiting?"

"Um, no." I shift, eyeing each of my men before reluctantly turning my attention back to the doctor. "I'm fine."

"How's your pain level? Some discomfort is to be expected with the type of head injury you've received. Look here." He motions for me to track his finger as he shines a light in my eyes, and I tense, pain sparking through my head.

"I'm fine," I repeat, as if saying it enough times will make it true, and follow the rest of his instructions as he continues his exam.

"Amour," Xander scolds me as Dr. Patel reaches forward, probing my forehead.

I jolt.

"You should be in bed, Ms. Beaumont," Dr. Patel scolds, his knowing eyes scanning my face. "I'll have the nurse bring you something for the pain."

"I-I said I was—"

"Flower," Rhys cuts in, and I sigh, dropping my gaze.

"I'd like to keep you here for observation, but once your pain is managed well with NSAIDs, we can discuss getting you discharged," Dr. Patel states, and I nod as he grumbles something under his breath. "I'd normally prefer to speak with you *alone* but—"

I look up as he glances between my three men, and watch as he rolls his eyes.

"I suppose leaving their line of sight is out of the question?"

"For now," Everett confirms and I shift, anxiety swelling in my gut.

Why does he want to talk to me alone?

Is there something wrong with me?

Am I sick?

"Ms. Beaumont, I was informed by another physician that there was concern you'd been sexually assaulted."

Oh. I tense as my face heats with embarrassment, and for the first time since my capture, I find myself wishing that I was anywhere but *here* beneath the Grimm Brothers' gazes.

"We can offer you medications to protect against any diseases that may have been transmitted during—"

"I-I wasn't—" I pause in my interruption, but only long enough to swallow around the lump in my throat. "I wasn't raped."

My entire body is rigid, tight with anxiety as memories from the shower assault me, but if Dr. Patel notices, he doesn't pry. "If you need anything, you can have one of the nurses reach out to me, all right?"

I thank him as he stands to make his way to the door.

"I'm serious, Mr. Grimm. Not one foot out of bed, am I clear?" he tosses the reminder over his shoulder, and waits until Xander nods, before he eyes me again. "And you need to get back to bed, Ms. Beaumont. You both need rest."

I try to nod, but with the pounding in my skull and my racing thoughts, I'm not sure if I manage the movement.

"Flower...?" Rhys gently strokes my arm once the doctor is gone, and I blink, forcing my eyes up to him. "We should get you back."

I know my men won't push me to explain what happened, but I can see the worry carved onto each of their faces. I know how it must have looked, finding me wet and in his clothes, but I don't know that I'm ready to unpack everything that happened.

"I-I'm sorry, I..." I trail off, and bite my lip, unsure how to explain.

"Don't apologize, pet," Everett murmurs.

I sigh, my mouth opening and closing as a response builds and just as quickly evaporates from my tongue.

"It's okay, Amour," Xander muses from his place in the bed, and I look to him, feeling insecure. "We're here when you're ready."

I nod as Xander's blue eyes slide between his brothers, and find myself on the outside of their silent conversation. One day, I'll figure out how to decode their unspoken language, but today...

"Go and get some rest, Amour. You need it," Xander says, jutting his chin toward the door.

I frown and shake my head. "I don't want to —"

"You heard Dr. Patel, Flower." Rhys' reminder makes me roll my eyes.

"That's twice now, pet." Everett's low hiss makes me flush despite the fear and pain coiling through me. A small giggle comes from the back of my throat, surprising me, as I scan Everett's face. "Yes, I'm counting."

"Don't worry, Flower. We won't let him spank you until you're a little less fragile." Rhys' words make everyone laugh, including Xander, who's quick to break out into a fit of coughing.

He flinches, his shoulders curling as he tries to catch his breath, and Everett curses.

"Xander." I lean forward, wanting to help, but he holds up his hand.

"I-I'm good." He chokes out, his breath shaky as he clears his throat. "I'm good."

I eye him skeptically, but he offers me a small smile that manages to ease the worry in my chest.

"Go on, Amour. You heard Patel, I'm not going anywhere. Go get some rest."

Everett tugs the wheelchair back before I can raise another rebuttal, and I grumble as I'm taken from the room. Crossing my arms, I make Rhys promise that I can return after my short nap. I hadn't been ready to admit it in the room, but I am exhausted. I slump into the bed as my men get me situated, and soon after, a nurse arrives with my pain medications. She does her standard checks while I take the pills she's provided, and I convince her to disconnect the IV line since I'm able to take clear liquids.

"I'll have the kitchen bring up some chicken broth for you to start on in a little bit. As long as you can keep that down, you shouldn't need any more fluids through here." She taps the IV pump, and motions to the call button behind me. "If you need us, just press that, okay?"

"Thanks." I nod, and lean back into the bed as she disappears.

Rhys pulls the blankets up over me and settles into the chair beside my bed. Everett hovers by the window, scouring the rising sun in the distance, his lips pressed into a thin line.

"Sleep, Flower. You need it," Rhys murmurs.

With the warmth of the blankets around me, and the pain medication quickly working through my system, I'm no match for the exhaustion that pulls me under.

Chapter Thirty-Five

Rhys

Brielle drifts off without another word, her body going limp against the mattress as sleep takes her away from her pain. I sigh and brush a stray strand of hair away from her face.

"Sam's settling in okay." My words stir Everett, who's hovering beside the window. He turns to raise a brow at me, so I continue. "We're lucky Mrs. Claebourne has a son around his age. It sounds like he's been helping him open up a bit."

He crosses the room toward us and sits down into his designated chair, his hand reaching out to stroke along the cast encircling her wrist.

"It's going to take him time, though. He's pretty shut down," I murmur, praying that in her sleep, Brielle can't hear me.

If she knew that her brother wasn't doing well mentally, that he was scared and afraid, I'm not sure she'd ever rest again.

"Who wouldn't be after everything that's happened? They're *both* going to need time," Everett confirms, his fingers gently tapping against the plaster.

I frown and nod as I scan Brielle, knowing his words are true. We'd heard the pain in her voice, the discomfort that laced her tone when she'd denied being raped. He may not have forced himself on her, but *something* happened. If that wasn't clear enough from the way that we found her, half-naked and wet, then her reaction to Dr. Patel's question provided more than enough proof of that. She hasn't been ready to discuss what happened, but I pray that one day, she'll share with at least *one* of us before it tears her apart.

"He keeps asking Mrs. Claebourne when you'll be back," I say, looking over her sleeping figure at him.

He winces. "I can't leave…"

Guilt darkens his face, and I know it must be difficult. The kid seems to have latched onto him, despite the instance in which Sammy first saw him. Kidnapping his sister. I know that he wants to be with him, helping him cope in whatever way he can, but he can't be in two places at once.

No one can.

Brielle is a testament to that. She's spent her entire adult life trying to live for herself and Samuel. Hopefully, we can find a way to give her the freedom she needs to choose where she wants to be for herself.

"Brielle needs me here. Xander needs me here. I *can't* leave," he repeats the last words, as if needing me to confirm their validity.

"You could always bring him here to visit Brielle? I'm sure it would do them both some good. Besides, you could use a break. When you run him home, you might be able to get some decent sleep." I motion to his head, but he rolls his eyes, and flicks me off.

"I'm not the only one with a head injury, Rhys," he mutters.

"Sure, but there's a pretty big difference between some burned, grazed skin and a bruised fucking *brain*, Everett," I curse.

"If you don't drop it, I'm going to give you an injury to match mine," he threatens with a smirk.

I chuckle, and as our laughter begins spilling into the room, a knock sounds on the door.

"I'm sorry to interrupt but" — a nurse peeks around the corner, her eyes jumping between the two of us, and Brielle — "she really needs her rest, and we can hear you two laughing in the hall."

"Shit, sorry."

"Sorry."

We're quick to apologize. She nods, satisfied that she's chastised us well, before she disappears again. Once the door clicks shut behind her, we both burst into quiet, hissed laughter again.

"We're going to get kicked out," I chuckle.

"I'd like to see them try." Everett smiles and shakes his head as he leans back in his chair. "We should shut up, though. Brielle needs her rest."

"I'll go sit with Xander. You stay here," I offer, standing. "Text me once she's up, all right?"

"Yeah." He nods.

Turning away from them, I head toward the door, dropping my gaze.

I'm fucking exhausted.

With the weeks of non-stop hunting and searching for Draven behind us, the continuous running is beginning to weigh on me. Maybe I can get some sleep while the two patients rest. I smirk, heading down the hall toward Xander's room.

If only.

* * * *

Everett

"Here you go, love. If you can keep this down, I'll talk with the physician about clearing you for solids, all right?"

"Thank you."

Brielle's gentle voice floats through my head, and I forgo attempting to fall into what I'm sure would be an unsatisfying sleep. I groan and sit up, my neck tight with pain.

"I'm sorry. I didn't mean to wake you." Brielle frowns, eyeing me as I attempt to rub away the knot that's formed in my muscles.

"You didn't, pet. I wasn't able to drift off." I reply.

There's a bowl of broth sitting in front of her, but instead of reaching for the spoon, she reaches for me.

"Come up here so you can sleep." She traces a finger over my wrinkled forehead, and tries shifting to make room.

When she winces, I grab her shoulder and stand, forcing her to stall in her efforts. "Brielle, don't. I'm okay."

"Y-You look—"

"Pet," I interrupt, and jut a chin toward her forgotten food. "Don't worry about me. Just eat, please."

She lifts her broken hand instinctively, but stops, her frown deepening as she remembers she can no longer use her dominant hand.

Fucker.

I pick up the spoon before she can move to use her opposite hand. "Let me help you, pet."

"I can do it…" she murmurs.

"I know." I scoop up a spoonful of the broth and hold it to her lips. "I just want to help."

She opens her mouth and accepts the broth, swallowing with a low moan. "God. I didn't realize how hungry I was."

I feed her another bite and grit my teeth, doing my best to ignore the sound of her pleasure as she eats. She finishes the bowl, and within an hour, the nurse has her cleared for solids.

Rhys comes into the room to sit with her, and helps her eat some of the turkey sandwich that's been brought up from the cafeteria. She jokes about the bread being soggy, and says that she wishes she had some of Mrs. Claebourne's cooking instead, but she finishes that tray of food, too.

"Xander is awake," Rhys tells me as she settles back into her bed. "He wants to see you, whenever you've got a second."

I glance down at Brielle, whose eyes are fluttering as she struggles to stay awake. "Go. Tell him I said 'hi'."

She smiles, and I kiss her forehead as she drifts back off to sleep.

"I'll be down the hall if you need me," I whisper to her, and eye Rhys. "Let me know once she's awake."

He tosses a salute at me as I go.

Chapter Thirty-Six

Xander

The pain is tolerable.

What *isn't* tolerable is being confined to this *fucking* bed.

"I want off bedrest," I grit through my teeth, and the nurse beside me rolls her eyes.

"Dr. Patel was clear, Mr. Grimm." The response is one that I've heard numerous times, from every single medical person that comes in here.

It doesn't mean I stop asking.

She tugs the blood pressure cuff off my arm and checks my oxygen saturation for the sixth time since she's stepped into the room. She puts the reading down into my chart, and darts toward the door as Everett walks into the room.

"He's not allowed out of bed," she squeaks to him before disappearing into the hall.

He cocks his brow at me as he leans against the wall, smirking. "Causing trouble, Beast?"

I roll my eyes, and cough. "Always."

He chuckles under his breath and lowers himself into the seat beside me, his brown eyes roving over the wires and tubes trapping me to the bed. "How're you feeling?"

"I'm—"

"No bullshit, Xander. I know you too well," he interrupts, and I grit my teeth.

"It fucking sucks." I pull in a sharp inhale, and gesture toward my chest. "It's like breathing in b-broken glass."

He nods, frowning. "It'd suck less if you'd take the pain meds they keep offering you."

"I can't be drugged out. Brielle—"

"Is *safe*. Safe for the first real time in months, and she needs you to get better so you can get out of here." He mutters an apology under his breath when I raise a brow at him. "Oh, and she says 'hi'."

She's *safe*.

After months of struggling to find her threat, after countless nights of missed sleep, she's finally *safe*.

Because Draven Augustin is dead.

If only her life could return to normal.

"Have you heard any news on George?" I ask, clearing my throat.

He shakes his head. "There's not been any change. His doctor doesn't seem optimistic."

"Fuck," I curse.

"Fuck is right," Everett confirms, and eyes me. "She doesn't need you prolonging your stay because you're stubborn. She needs you better."

"Really, with the guilt trip, Everett?" I growl.

He shrugs and smirks. "Is it working?"

I sigh and press the call button, allowing the sharp sound of it trilling through the room to respond for me.

I'd *like* to kick his ass, to remind him who's in charge of our little family, but I swallow my pride and settle back against the bed as a nurse appears.

"You feeling okay, Mr. Grimm?" The nurse comes to my bedside and presses a button as she scans me.

"He's ready for some pain meds," Everett explains, and reaches over, gently patting my shoulder as the nurse leaves to retrieve my medication. "You're a good man, Beast. A *better* man."

"You only have one person to thank for that." I smile.

Brielle.

Brielle *fucking* Beaumont.

My woman.

Our woman.

"She's eating solids. There's talk about discharging her in a few days," Everett informs me.

"Good. She needs to get out of here. *I* need to get out of here," I grumble, and he rolls his eyes.

"You're not going anywhere anytime soon, Mr. Grimm." Dr. Patel rounds into the room with the nurse who disappeared to get the pain meds. "Or did you already forget what I said about updated imaging and bed rest?"

"I'm in bed." I grunt.

"And harassing every nurse that comes in about getting *out* of it." He comes to stand beside the bed, and passes me a small plastic cup.

I tip the pill back, and swallow it dry. "Thanks."

"Your blood pressure is up. What will it take for you to get some rest? Do I need to knock you out?" Dr. Patel questions, flipping through my chart.

Everett laughs, and as our eyes slide to him, he nods. "I know something that might help."

Chapter Thirty-Seven

Brielle

"You're sure Dr. Patel said this was okay?" I question, skeptical.

The room is quiet, aside from the light beep of monitors, and the gentle whoosh of oxygen. It's rhythmic, and despite my recent nap, might be enough to lull me back to sleep.

"Yes, I'm sure, Flower." Rhys, who's positioned himself on the edge of my bed, strokes his long fingers across my knee. "Everett figured it was the best way to keep him in bed."

My eyes drift to the sleeping figure lying in the hospital bed beside mine, and I smile as a light snore rumbles from his chest.

My Beast.

He stayed awake long enough to watch the nurses maneuver my bed into the room, but as soon as I was positioned beside him, the pain meds took him under.

He'd tried fighting it at first, his eyelids fluttering open and closed for a few moments, before he finally succumbed. I'm grateful that at least one of my men is getting the sleep he needs.

I slide my eyes back to Rhys, and raise a brow. "What about you? What will it take to get you in bed?"

He waggles his eyebrows at me mischievously. "You know I love you, Flower, but I don't think you're in any condition to — "

"That's not what I meant." I smack his arm lightly with my good hand, and he chuckles. "You need sleep, too."

"These hospital chairs are comfortable enough to snag a few minutes here and there." He smirks, trying to lighten the worry weighing me down.

It doesn't work. "I can make room. Or maybe we can ask for a rollaway bed or something."

"I'm all right, Flower. I promise," he assures me.

"I just want everything to go back to normal. *Our* normal." I sigh.

He laughs, and squeezes my hand gently. "Everett and I will sleep better once you're both home, that's for sure."

"Is he okay?" I question, glancing toward the cracked door.

Everett stepped into the hall with Dr. Patel after overseeing my room change, and hasn't been back yet.

"Dr. Patel is just giving him a once-over. He got knocked out cold by that fucker guarding your dad, and left before anyone had the chance to check his head," Rhys explains.

Now my eyes dart toward the injury tracked across the side of *his* head, a graze burn left behind by a bullet. They haven't explained the story of how he received the injury, and while I'm not sure I'm ready to hear it, the sight is still enough to make my stomach coil.

"I owe you three everything," I whisper.

Rhys' green eyes meet mine, and he frowns, no doubt sensing my worry. He reaches forward and gently cups my face, his thumb soft as he strokes my cheek.

"*You* are our everything, Brielle." His soft words make my face heat. "There's nothing else we could ever want."

I lean forward, ignoring the pain that sparks in my ribs. "I love you."

"I love you," he repeats against my lips.

He's gentle, far gentler than he's ever been as he pulls me closer, his lips moving against mine. The feeling makes me moan, and I shift forward, desperate to feel him against me.

"Rhys." A warning comes from behind us, and I sigh as he breaks the kiss. "What was our agreement?"

We both watch as Everett seals the door behind him before crossing the room, his brown orbs heated with disapproval as he eyes us with a raised brow.

"We agreed to wait," Rhys mutters in reply.

Wait? Wait for what?

"I was gone for ten minutes," Everett scolds, smirking as he lowers himself into a nearby chair.

Rhys waves him off and scoots back, giving me space I neither want nor need. "And? How's your head?"

"It'll be fine," Everett replies.

"Hang on. What just happened?" I question, looking between the two men.

Everett eyes Rhys for a moment before shaking his head. "It's nothing, pet."

"You said you 'agreed to wait'. What does that mean?" I ask.

Rhys sighs and shifts. "We wanted to give you time to heal before...initiating anything."

"I'm not broken." I try to cross my arms, but my cast gets in the way, refuting my coarse words. I growl and drop my hands into my lap, frustrated. "I think I am more than capable of deciding for myself whether or not I'm well enough for certain *activities*."

"Yes, but that doesn't mean—"

A low groan rumbles through the room, cutting Everett's words short. We all look toward Xander as he peels his eyes open a crack, just enough to scan his brothers, before he shuts them again.

"Kiss. Don't kiss. Let the woman do what she wants, just do it quietly. I'm trying to rest so I can get the fuck out of here." He grumbles the panted, broken words without reopening either eye.

I can't help the small giggle that escapes me as we all murmur apologies for the noise.

Raising a brow, I glance between Rhys and Everett mischievously. "So?"

"I've said it once, and I'll say it again Rhys, I am not above punishing you." Everett hisses.

I shoot him a look, but he just smirks and holds up two fingers, a reminder that he's still counting my digressions.

I *almost* roll my eyes.

"Let's give it a few more days, Flower." Rhys strokes the back of my hand, and I nod, conceding.

"Now that's a good girl, pet," Everett murmurs.

I slide my narrowed eyes to him. "Don't test me, Brass."

He holds up his hands, and again, we break out into laughter. Xander grunts and, unsure if it's another complaint of the noise, we all quiet ourselves.

"You should get some more rest, too," Rhys whispers and juts his chin toward the pillows beckoning me to revisit them.

"Fine," I mutter, knowing there's no point in fighting. They just want what's best for me, and I *am* tired.

I lie back and allow Everett to reposition one pillow behind my head with little to no complaint. Rhys flips off the reading light beside my bed, and lowers the curtains, casting the room into semi-darkness. I drift before he's retaken his seat beside me.

Chapter Thirty-Eight

Everett

Brielle shifts in the bed as she adjusts her hair —
again — and I frown.

"You look beautiful, pet," I murmur, settling onto
the bed beside her.

I can sense the unease sparking through her as she
waves off my compliment, can see it in the way she
worries her lip between her teeth and furrows her
brow. She's nervous, and her fear is making my
stomach coil with uncertainty.

Maybe this is a mistake.

"I-I just don't want the bruising to freak him out —"

"Everett and Mrs. Claebourne told him that you
have some injuries, Flower. He understands as much as
any kid can." Rhys tries to soothe her, but the crease
between her brows only deepens.

"He's just going to be happy to see you, pet," I
reassure her, stroking a hand down her arm. She nods,

but despite the small acknowledgment, I'm not sure that she truly believes me. "We don't have to do a video call if you're not ready. I'm sure he'd be fine just hearing your —"

"No, no. It's fine. It's just...so much has changed, since I last saw him. *I've* changed. I just don't want..." She trails off and shrugs, unsure of how to voice her fear.

"Baby steps, Flower. It's going to take time." Rhys juts his chin toward the phone in her hand and smiles at her encouragingly.

"He's your family, Brielle. It'll never matter how much you change, or what you do. He's always going to love you," I remind her, and click on the app that will allow her to call her brother. "When you're ready, just hit this."

I show her the number to dial — Mrs. Claebourne's — and stand.

"We'll be right outside," Rhys tells her.

She looks between us, a soft, sad smile pulled onto her lips. "Thank you. I love you both."

"I love you, pet."

"I love you too, Flower."

The sound of the line ringing echoes through the room as we step into the hall, and before we can shut the door, the call connects.

"Bri?" Sam's voice booms through the speakers, and I pause as Brielle sniffles. "Bri, it's you!"

"H-Hi, Sammy." Her voice cracks my chest open, and it takes everything I have not to run back into the room to make sure that she's okay.

Gritting my teeth, I shut the door, praying that if she does need us, she'll call out. I sigh and lean against the wall.

"She'll be okay," Rhys states, although when I glance his way, I can't decide if he's speaking more to me, or himself.

He's pacing, his hands tugging through his tangled mop of curls as he scans the hall. Other than a few nurses scattered here and there, the place is mostly empty. Visiting hours ended earlier this evening, and while I'm sure the nurses would like a break from us, our status ensures we're left alone. No one messes with the Grimm Brothers, and now that Draven is out of the way, there will be no one messing with our woman, either.

"She *will* be okay." My words make Rhys pause, and he sighs before coming to stand beside me.

"What if she wants to leave? I can't imagine that our lifestyle is one she wants to thrust her brother into..." He shakes his head, and pinches the bridge of his nose. "Or what if she stays? What if she stays, but wants to have kids someday? What kind of life would we be giving our—"

"Rhys." I turn on him and grab his shoulder roughly, hoping that the sharp bite of my touch will ground him and still his racing thoughts. It seems to work. He blows out a breath, inhales for a beat, then releases another sharp exhale. Stealing his words from earlier, I continue. "Baby steps, Blaze."

He chuckles sheepishly, but nods. "I guess we should worry about getting her discharged first, hm?"

"Yes. Her and Xander, eventually." I scan the hall, searching for our brother.

Dr. Patel made another round earlier this evening, and noticed some rattling in Xander's lungs. While that could be normal, given the extent of his injury, he wanted to ensure he wasn't developing something like pneumonia. A few nurses took him for X-rays right before we set Brielle up for her call, but he's not back yet.

I suppose that's a good thing.

She deserves her privacy.

"It's just a few days away. She'll be home, and we'll have a kid living with us," Rhys murmurs.

His words make my back straighten. "Fuck. We'll have to do some work on the house before Sam gets there."

My mind drifts to the basement, so easily accessible, and Rhys laughs.

"What happened to 'baby steps'?" he teases.

"That's different and you —"

"Guys?" Brielle calls, interrupting my train of thought.

Rhys is quick to push through the door, and I follow close on his heel. The phone is sitting in Brielle's lap, and although her eyes are rimmed with tears, a smile lights up her face.

"He had to go. Noah had some new video game to show him." She blows out a breath and reaches for me.

I take her hand, and allow her to pull me down onto the edge of her bed. "Pet?"

"Thank you." She wraps her arms around my neck so quickly I all but fall into her embrace. "Thank you, thank you, thank you for getting him out of there safely."

I hug her back as gently as I can, and kiss the side of her head.

"Anything for you, Brielle. Always."

Chapter Thirty-Nine

Brielle

I don't think I'm ready.

I lean back against the seat and bite my lip, my eyes darting across the world waiting just beyond the windows for me.

I'm not ready...

"Don't forget to breathe, pet," Everett whispers, and tucks a stray strand of hair behind my ear. "Just breathe."

I allow his touch to ground me for a moment and pull in a steadying breath.

"You sound like your brother," I quip, a small smile tugging onto my lips.

"That's good. He's the one who told me what to say," he replies with a light chuckle.

I turn my gaze back toward the window, and scan the home waiting for me. My brother is inside somewhere, anxiously awaiting my arrival. I reach for the handle, but pause as fear snakes its way into my stomach.

What if I've changed too much?

"Ready, Flower?" Rhys turns to look at us from the driver's seat, his eyebrows quirked above his green orbs.

No.

I nod my head.

Count, Brielle.

Rhys slides out of the front seat as Everett pushes our door open and outstretches his hand for me to take.

One.

I place my hand into his and slowly follow behind him as he slips from the car.

Two.

The movement jostles me, and I wince despite my desperation to keep the pain I'm still in concealed.

Three.

"Take it slow, pet," Everett murmurs, catching my discomfort before I'm able to tamp it down.

Four.

I pull in a short breath and nod, steadying myself as I take a hesitant step toward the house.

Five.

Rhys falls into place on my opposite side, and with their bodies beside me, some of my fear eases.

Six.

Climbing the steps isn't as painful as I'd anticipated, and we get to the door faster than I'm prepared for.

Seven.

Everett reaches forward, and as he pushes it open, the familiar beep of the alarm system pings through the foyer.

Eight.

I step into the house behind him as footsteps thunder against the hardwood.

Nine.

"Brielle!" Sammy's voice drowns out the sound of his racing steps, and then he's there, rounding the corner.

Ten.

His brown curls bounce as he runs, and tears spark in my eyes as his small body collides with mine, nearly doubling me over.

"Sammy." I wrap my arms around him and tug him close, holding him firmly against me despite the pain lancing through my ribs. "God, Sam…"

He sniffles, and I pull away, just enough to scan his face. His eyes are wet with unshed tears, but he doesn't let them fall.

Instead, he giggles and wrinkles his nose. "You smell like a hospital."

I scoff, and hug him again, a sad laugh breaking through my lips.

"Yeah? I guess I'd better shower then." I sigh and press the side of my face against his hair, frowning. "You're taller."

"You think so?" He pulls away excitedly, and twists, as if doing so will show off his newly grown inches.

I roll my eyes and laugh. "Definitely. You're really going to need some new clothes, now."

My mind drifts back to the day I'd been taken by the Grimm Brothers and the seemingly insignificant worries I'd had at the time. Going through Sammy's clothes to see what would last him through the winter. Finding a job.

That seems like a lifetime ago…

"I already have new clothes." Sammy shrugs, and gestures behind him. "Do you want to see? They're in my room."

"Your...your room?" My confusion doesn't faze Sam as he bounces backward with a grin.

"Come on! I'll show you. Mrs. Claire and Noah are helping me put them away." He runs off before I can form any other words, and I'm left staring, baffled, at my two men.

"I-I don't understand..." I trail off, my eyes following the direction my little brother has just raced off in.

"You're ours, Brielle, and this is your home. We'd never ask you to live away from Sam," Everett whispers, his hand gentle as it takes mine.

"We started getting everything ready for him once we finalized your discharge date. The clothes were just delivered this morning," Rhys explains, and I reel, my heart thumping in my chest.

"You got a room ready for him in two days?" I ask, bewildered.

Rhys nods, a smirk on his lips as he leads us forward. "There's still some work that needs done, but it's a start."

"He got to pick the paint and a bedspread that matched. Xander wasn't thrilled with the color choice, but it's not his room." Everett chuckles.

"Xander's in on this, too?" I whisper.

"It was his idea," Rhys confirms.

I try to figure out when in the last two days they'd have had the time to do this. Without me knowing. Xander and I shared a room until the day I was released...they would have had to do all their planning while I slept. Which means...

"How are you two still standing?" They haven't slept well in *weeks*.

"Caffeine," they both reply.

We turn down the back hallway, and I pause for a moment, my eyes drifting toward the basement door.

"It'll stay locked until we have a chance to remodel," Everett assures me, and I release a small breath.

"Remodel?" I whisper as we inch toward the open door where laughter and voices are spilling from.

"Xander doesn't want you or Sam living in a house with...well..." Rhys trails off, and I know what he's thinking without him having to voice the words.

A torture room.

"Bri! Come on!" Sam calls for me, and I take the few steps needed to round into his room.

His room.

The thought makes me smile, and as I scan the space, I realize why Xander must've disliked the choice in color for the room. It's a bright blue, similar to the color of his eyes, and is far from the neutral shades that fill the rest of the house.

"Welcome home, dear." Mrs. Claebourne smiles from where she stands at the closet, hanging clothes, and I nod a small 'hello' to her.

Sam is going through a pile of T-shirts that are laid on the bed, and he holds up a red basketball tee with a goofy grin.

"Look at this one, Bri." He waves me over, and just like that, the part of me I'd been worried was too far gone falls back into place.

But I no longer feel like his mother.

Now, I'm just his sister.

As I always should have been.

"Show me everything."

Chapter Forty

Rhys

Over the next week, we fall into a fairly comfortable routine. Sammy is always the first one in the house to wake, and he somehow managed to familiarize himself with the theater room within his first few days in the home. Every morning, once we've managed to rouse ourselves, we're sure to find him watching cartoons or sitting on the floor, right in front of the flat screen, playing whatever video game has snagged his attention.

Brielle felt guilty about it at first. She's spent his entire life waking before him to ensure they were always on time, and it's foreign, sleeping in with him in the home. I, for one, am grateful that he's comfortable enough to find entertainment in our home, on his own. It gives Brielle, and *us*, the time we need to catch up on the sleep we lost over the past month of hell.

By the time we wake, and help Brielle get herself ready — she still needs some assistance washing, dressing and fixing her hair — Mrs. Claebourne has normally arrived with her son, Noah. It's a new arrangement, one that we had to come up with on the spot with Sammy's arrival, but it seems to be working in his favor. Noah helps keep him grounded in a world that — *I'm sure* — feels out of control, with things that seem normal to kids their age. Complaints about homework. Worries about cooties. What shoes are 'in style' and which aren't. Stupid things that neither of my brothers or I had the privilege of experiencing.

While they're keeping each other busy, Mrs. Claebourne and I make breakfast, and Everett updates her on Xander's condition. Brielle normally hovers with us in the kitchen, drinking coffee and making small talk with Claire, but her ears are always listening for her brother in case he calls her. Once breakfast is finished, Mrs. Claebourne takes Noah to school. Sammy has been tagging along with her the past few days, although we haven't enrolled him yet. Brielle thought it best to give him more time to adjust, but going with Mrs. Claebourne allows him to get familiarized with the area and the routine.

In the short time that he's gone, we call Xander to check in. Brielle does most of the talking — Beast has never been a morning person, and is more tolerant with her asking the questions — and updates him on what's going on at home. Mostly, she talks about Sammy. It's an easy topic, one that doesn't bring up *her* or her injuries. Everett and I have noticed the reluctance to discuss them, even when we're helping her and accidentally touch a tender spot. We don't want to push her, but we haven't been able to figure out the best way to approach it yet, either.

By the time Mrs. Claebourne has arrived back with Sammy, it's normally an acceptable time to visit the hospital. We always stop by their father first. Sammy doesn't really understand that the machines are the reason their father continues breathing, but Brielle's done her best to shield him from the scarier side of his prognosis. A prognosis that will result in death, if he doesn't make progress, soon.

Thankfully, waking up is the only thing George has left to conquer. Like Conrad, Draven managed to pay the officer George assaulted to ensure he pressed charges instead of releasing a drug ridden Beaumont to a hospital or rehab facility for treatment. After the money stopped coming, and Xander got involved, the assault and drug charges disappeared. He's a free man.

He just needs to wake up.

We spend most of the day with him. Our woman seems happiest when all three of us are with her, but it's hard, with her little brother in tow. He doesn't understand our relationship. It's one that not many *can* understand, but it's especially difficult when his idea of family has been so misconstrued all these years. Brielle can't keep being his motherly figure, if she's going to live for herself...and I *do* hope she starts living for herself.

"Are you okay, Rhys?" Brielle's tired mumble rises through the darkness, pulling me out of my thoughts. "Is it the storm?"

Thunder is rattling the roof above us, but with her nestled beside me, it's easy to ignore.

"I'm okay, Flower. Go back to sleep." I lean down and kiss her forehead, and she murmurs something soft under her breath.

This is how we end our days. After getting home from the hospital, it's always a whirlwind of eating, spending time with Sam, and getting him ready for bed. We always collapse into her bed, Everett on one side, me on the other with her cradled in between us. It's the best fucking part of my day, and it always gets cut short by me dozing off. I just want to hold her, and never let her go.

Her hand drags up my chest, the plaster protecting her broken wrist scratching along my skin, and she sighs. "I can't wait to get this dumb thing off."

"You're supposed to be going back to sleep," I scold, gently laying my hand on top of hers.

"I know," she whispers. Her fingers move, delicately tracing along my chest before she continues. "What're you thinking about?"

I chuckle. "You."

"What about me?" She scoots, adjusting herself so that she can peer at me through the dark.

Her nose touches my jaw as she looks up at me, and the heat of her exhale brushes against my neck. With her body so close to mine, it's difficult to ignore my cock as it stirs to life in my shorts.

Not now.

"Mostly just how good it feels having you lying against me." I can't keep the gravel out of my voice, and I bite back a groan as she stiffens beside me.

Don't push her, Blaze.

"It's been really hard..." She pauses, and I worry that she's thinking about whatever happened with

Draven before she continues. "Behaving myself when I'm in bed with you two."

Oh, fuck me.

"Flower—"

"I know, I know," she interrupts, rolling onto her back. "You guys are just worried about hurting me, but I'm not as fragile as I look. The pain's hardly even been noteworthy the last few days."

"Brielle…"

I push myself onto my elbow so I can look down at her. It's dark, but there's enough light coming in from the full moon that I can make out her delicate features. Her full lips. Her delicate nose. The bruises still darkening her skin.

How can I explain? She's not fragile, we know, but she *is* breakable. We don't want to spark any pain, to her injuries or her mind. She still hasn't told us what happened with Draven. We're terrified of doing something that might mentally take her back to that.

"Please?" She moves now, her left hand reaching out to grab my dick. "I want you."

Well fuck.

Goodbye, self-control.

Chapter Forty-One

Brielle

I can feel his length through the thin material of his shorts, and I moan softly, desperate. It's felt like *years* since I've had any of my men, and the deprivation has only worsened my desire for them.

My *need*.

I maneuver my hand past the elastic waistband keeping him from me and continue my path until the head of his cock brushes against my fingertips.

"Flower, are you sure you're—" His words turn into a low hiss as I gently slide my hand down his length, reveling in the hardness. "Fucking hell."

His head drops back against the pillow and I smile, pleased, as I wrap my hand around the base of his dick. I'm slow as I stroke him, gliding my fist smoothly up and down, up and down, hardening him further beneath my ministrations. It makes my breath catch, and I squirm as desire floods my belly.

"Is that good, Blaze?" I whisper.

A low moan comes from the back of his throat in response and the sound drives me to pump him faster.

I want to hear that sound again.

Need to hear that sound again...

A hand snakes around my waist from behind, and I still as a growl heats the shell of my ear. "Misbehaving, pet?"

Everett moves, sitting up behind me, and I bite my lip, nervous. I haven't been cleared by Dr. Patel to do any *extracurricular* activities yet, but surely enough time has passed...

Please don't make me stop.

"I might be, sir," I muse.

I glance at him over my shoulder and toss a sweet smile in his direction as I resume my *misbehavior*.

"Mmm..." He nips at my lobe, and presses his own budding erection against me. "You're lucky I'm in a forgiving mood tonight, pet."

He kisses my jaw, and as I slide my thumb through the pre-cum collecting at Rhys' tip, his tongue drags down my neck. I shiver as he bites me, his teeth brandishing enough pain to stir a light yelp from me before he soothes it away with his lips. It's titillating, and distracting enough that in my pause, Rhys has the time to remove his shorts.

"You'll tell us if something hurts, Flower?" Rhys cups my cheek, turning my face up to his while Everett continues biting and kissing my neck.

"Yes."

The word is barely past my lips before he's kissing me, his tongue invading my mouth in a searing, claiming kiss. It's intense, the need behind his touch, and I melt into him as Everett's hand slides into my shorts.

"Fuck, pet. You're soaked." Everett's words escape on a harsh exhale as he cups me through my underwear, and I writhe, my entire body quivering with need.

I whine into Rhys' mouth, gasping as his tongue strokes against mine.

I needed this.

I needed them.

Everett's fingers skim over the damp spot that's collected in my panties, teasing me, and again, I whimper.

"Please." My plea is nearly unintelligible as our lips clash together, but Everett chuckles, hearing me.

"You want me to touch you, pet?" He tugs my baggy shirt aside enough to bite my shoulder, and I nod as much as I'm able. "Hm?"

Now, I break the kiss. "Yes. Yes, sir. Please."

His hand moves, rising enough to trace along the hem of my underwear, but he doesn't dip beneath the fabric. I groan and drop my head back against his chest, my skin burning with heat as he slowly traces the line of my panties.

"You'd better give our woman what she wants, brother," Rhys warns, eyeing Everett over my shoulder.

"It's just so enjoyable, hearing her beg for my touch." Everett snickers.

He presses a gentle kiss to my temple and, finally, slides his hand beneath the fabric separating us.

"Yes." I gasp and buck my hips, desperate, as his fingers dip between my folds.

Please.

Fuck, please.

"Greedy girl." His breath is hot against my ear as he circles my entrance, and I wiggle in his hold, my hips mirroring his movements.

"Everett." I'm panting, my breath coming in uneven gasps. "Please."

When the tip of his finger pushes forward, sliding inside me, I nearly come apart at the seams.

I mewl, arching back as he begins finger-fucking me. It's a slow, gentle pace at first, allowing my pussy to stretch around his digit before he picks up speed.

"You're so tight, pet." His praise makes my body heat, and he chuckles as he pushes another finger into me.

My mouth waters as he spears me, his fingers curling to stroke along the spot that will make me come. I'm close before he's really begun, my stomach coiling as the orgasm builds deep within my belly.

My eyes drift, floating to where Rhys is knelt, watching with an amused smirk. He's stroking himself, his hand moves in long, leisurely strokes as he enjoys the show before him.

I need him.

I reach for him and he moves to close the small distance between us, sensing my need.

When my hand wraps around his cock and pumps, he jolts, a low hiss escaping through his clenched teeth. "Fuck, Flower."

I stroke him in time with the fingers sliding in and out of my pussy, my hips rolling to meet the thrusts of his hand. Unencumbered moans spill freely from my lips, and I scream out as Everett inches me closer to the edge.

"Come for us, pet." Everett's order is harsh in my ear, and a low groan follows as his thumb brushes against my clit. "Come for — "

My orgasm rips through me before he can utter another word, and I shatter like glass in his hold. My body quakes, and I collapse back against him as loud cries of pleasure flow like the feeling coursing through me. He doesn't stop stroking me, using his touch to drag out my pleasure until I'm a useless pile of jelly in his arms.

He chuckles, and Rhys kisses my temple. "Feel better, Flower?"

I nod, still dazed, reeling and panting, earning a light laugh from both men.

"Do you think you can sleep now, pet?" Everett wonders, cradling me delicately.

"Mm..." I shake my head. "Not yet."

"No?" Rhys frowns, and raises a brow.

I giggle, and look between them. "Nope. Now, it's your turn."

Chapter Forty-Two

Everett

It takes some convincing on Brielle's end to get Rhys and me to agree to her plan, despite the hard cocks yearning for her attention. Our number one concern is, and always will be, her safety and well-being. We'd do anything to keep her from hurting, and her *request* was putting us at risk of reigniting some of the pain she insists is better. So…we had to make some adjustments.

"You need to tell us the second you feel anything other than pleasure, do you understand, pet?"

She's looking at me over her shoulder, her legs on either side of my hips. Her clothes are gone, as are mine, and Rhys is kneeling by my head. She bites her lip and nods, scanning the both of us before she begins scooting into position.

"Be gentle with her, Blaze." My warning slices into the room, and comes across more threatening than I intend, but Rhys voices his understanding.

"Yes, sir." His voice is low, filled with a mixture of concern and desire, but I don't have time to focus on him.

Not when my woman's gloriously bare, and wet pussy is lowering over my face.

"Is this okay?" The heat of Brielle's words brush against my cock, and it jolts, straining for her attention.

I reach up and smack her ass, not hard enough to cause pain, but with just enough force to spread a sting across her skin. "You're fucking perfect, pet."

She squeaks, and her hips shimmy as a light giggle escapes from her lips.

It's a sound I'll never tire of hearing.

I smirk, and in the moment I allow myself to revel in the sight of her, Brielle takes her opportunity. She swallows me, almost to the base, and the unexpectedness of it makes my hips buck. A loud growl comes from deep in my chest, and I drop my head back, my eyes squeezed shut in pure ecstasy.

Fuck, I needed this.

She's slow to release me, her tongue trailing up the side of my shaft to protect it from her teeth before she sucks on the head. It's sensitive, and again, my body responds, moving in a desperate need to inch in deeper.

"Fuck, pet," I murmur.

She moans against me, and the vibrations only harden me further.

I'm not wasting another goddamn second.

I lift my head, enough to trail my tongue around her clit and down through her wet folds, and she gasps in surprise. Her hips press down, nudging her needy cunt closer, and I take full advantage of her proximity. I dip my tongue into her, tasting the sweetness of her recent climax, and feel her tighten around me as her pleasure spikes.

I growl and return my attention to her clit, gently circling it before I pull it into my mouth. The suction makes her buck, and her lips stall mid-descent around my shaft, as pleasure distracts her in her pursuit.

Just you wait, pet.

I only remove myself from our woman long enough to call out, "Take her, brother."

Rhys is quick to follow my command, lining himself up at her entrance and thrusting himself inside her. She moans and pushes herself back against him, allowing me the perfect angle to attack her clit.

"Oh, fuck!" Her words are a shrill cry as I gently clamp that sensitive bundle of nerves between my teeth, growling as her body bounces above me.

Rhys is groaning, already close himself from just a few quick thrusts, and I suck on her hard, careening her closer to the edge.

"Fuck, Flower," he curses, and again, she jostles, her hips bucking in a desperate need to get him deeper.

I don't relent. I keep a steady pressure around her, and stroke her slowly with the tip of my tongue, applying the perfect amount of pressure and friction. She mewls, and as her legs begin quivering above me, I feel the heat of her mouth surround me once more.

Fucking hell.

Fucking...

Fuck.

My cock throbs, and I can feel myself rushing toward climax as the two bodies above me dance along their own precarious ledges. I can't fight it. Can't stop the heat that collects in the base of my stomach, and blooms outward, exploding as my climax erupts through me. I groan against her and suck hard, rolling my tongue until she's crashing down with me. She moans loudly as she takes my seed, swallowing it all while riding through the waves of her own pleasure. It's exhilarating. It's sexy as fuck. And the sight is enough to bring Rhys down with us.

When we all collapse back into the bed, sweaty, spent and satisfied, I can't help but chuckle. Brielle sits up, her hooded eyes scanning me in through the darkness of the room.

"What's so funny, Brass?" she whispers.

Her fingers trail through my chest hair as she raises a brow, waiting for an answer.

"You're such a good fucking girl, pet," I murmur.

I cup her cheek and kiss her, unafraid of the salty taste that lingers on her tongue. When her head drops onto my chest, I sigh, satisfied, and cradle her as Rhys spoons her from behind.

"I love you, Brielle," I reply, kissing her head.

"I love you too, Everett."

Sated, it's not long before all three of us are drifting back into the warm embrace of sleep.

Chapter Forty-Three

Brielle

"I-I'm sorry?" I shake my head, as if doing so will clear the fog of uncertainty that's just settled in my brain. *Surely I misheard him.* "I don't understand —"

"He's been asking for you."

The physician gestures toward the closed door in front of me with an astonished smile, as if he's just as surprised to be delivering this news as I am hearing it. I want to move, but I can't. My entire body seems to be cemented to the floor.

"Amour...?" Xander squeezes my hand, and I blink, forcing my eyes up to him. "Do you want to go in?"

My Beast, still recovering from his injuries, was granted permission to make this trip with us only with the understanding that he's still *very* far from healed. Dr. Patel was hesitant to allow him to do this much walking, but Everett assured him that his brother would remain wheelchair bound unless absolutely necessary. Of course, though, Xander is Xander. He only stayed in the wheelchair long enough to get to this floor. As soon as he was near enough to our destination, he ditched the chair and walked me here, his hand in mine.

"Flower?" Rhys strokes my arm, and I bite my lip, unsure.

Sammy is laughing behind me, and when I glance back, I see that he and Everett are talking in not so quiet whispers. My brother seems to have attached himself to Everett, and the two planted themselves in a waiting area down the hall while the rest of us left to talk with the physician. I'd been told he had an update, but I hadn't realized how big of an update it would be.

As if sensing my gaze, Everett glances up and smiles, offering me a comforting glance, somehow understanding my need, despite our short distance.

"Yes. I-I'd like to go in." My voice is unsteady, but given the news I've just received, it's not unexpected.

My dad...

He's...*awake.*

Awake and *asking* for me.

"Do you want some privacy, Amour? We can stay —"

"No. No, come in with me." I squeeze his hand tighter and look to Rhys. "Please?"

"Of course, Flower." He nods.

It takes a few moments for me to muster the courage to take another step forward, but before I'm ready, my feet are carrying me into the hospital room. Although I've been here, visiting every day over the past few weeks since my rescue, the room seems different when a familiar smile finds me across the room.

Well...half-smile.

"Bri..." My father's voice is a slurred rasp that stumbles into the room, but still, it's one that I'd recognize anywhere.

It makes tears spring to my eyes, and I'm hesitant as I step toward his bed, guilt weighing me down.

"Dad...I..." A lump forms in my throat, and it takes a few swallows to dislodge it. "I'm so sorry that this happened."

"N-No, Bri." His face contorts as he tries unsuccessfully to frown, and an annoyed groan rumbles from his chest. "I-I can't—"

"It's okay." I release Xander's hand and move forward, hovering beside the bed. "Just try to relax. Getting stressed will only make it worse."

His mouth twitches, and I can see him trying hard to remain calm, despite the lack of response from half his face. The facial paralysis he's suffering with was caused by the stroke, and while it isn't as severe as other cases that I've seen, getting used to it can't be easy.

"Are you s-safe?" He struggles to form the words, and I know from experience that his body is betraying his brain.

The damage is stopping it from responding in the way that he wants.

He's eyeing the men behind me, and I can see the fear that lingers in his gaze.

"Yes. They saved me." I sit in the chair beside his bed and take his hand in mine. It's limp, and I can feel his muscles shaking with the effort. Despite his obvious discomfort, he looks relieved for a moment as he scans the three of us. That is, until the confusion settles in once again. "It's a long story, but I promise I'm safe. We're safe. Sammy's here, too."

"S-S..." He can't get the name out, but I nod my understanding.

"Yes. He's just outside in the hall," I explain.

A tear slips from his eye, and I grab a tissue to swipe it away.

"Do you want to see him?" I whisper, and watch as he nods, his head jerking in an unpracticed motion that will take time to remaster.

I glance over my shoulder, but before I can ask, Rhys is disappearing into the hallway.

"Draven?" The name, even when it's a broken slur, still makes me flinch.

Xander steps forward, and squeezes my shoulder lightly before addressing my father. "Draven Augustin is no longer a problem. You're never going to have to worry about him, or your children's safety, again."

"T-Thank—"

"Don't. Don't thank me." Xander shakes his head, quickly brushing off my father's building praise. "I'd do anything for your daughter."

My father doesn't get the chance to respond.

Sammy bounds into the room, all smiles and shouts of excitement. The kid nearly knocks over an IV pole in his haste to get to Dad's bedside.

"Dad! You're awake! How are you? Are they making you eat the gross hospital food?" He rambles on and on without giving our father a chance to respond.

Not that he'd be able to muster much of a reply.

"You doing okay, Amour?" Xander's voice is low enough to not disturb Sammuel and the story he's spewing about his new home.

He's watching me carefully, his ice-blue eyes scanning me as I nod. There may be a long road ahead for my father, and his recovery, but now, with him awake and alert, I feel like a weight's been lifted off my shoulders.

He's going to be okay.

He's going to live.

We're *all* going to live.

Chapter Forty-Four

Xander

It's been one month.

One month of blank, white hospital rooms.

One month of Dr. Patel, medications, nurses, X-rays, breathing treatments, and too many other fucking things to count.

One *fucking* month.

This day couldn't have come any sooner.

"Are you sure you're ready for this?" Everett questions, his brow raised as he watches me through his peripheral.

The asshole is lucky he's driving. If he weren't, I'm sure I could figure out more than a few ways to show him just how *ready* I am. Most of which involve my fist.

"Yes, I'm sure," I growl.

Shifting in my seat, I pull in a slow breath and release it, testing myself. It took longer than I anticipated to be weaned off the oxygen, and although

I've spent a week or so without it, it still feels weird breathing without a tube beneath my nose.

"It's different now." He steers the car into the driveway and shrugs his shoulders. "I thought living with Sam would be strenuous, but it's been a breeze. Everything's been easier, since Draven…" He trails off, and shakes his head before continuing. "Rhys and I have almost felt useless, without a thousand extra things to do."

"Don't worry. I'm sure I can find something to keep you boys busy." I chuckle and do my best to ignore the pang of worry that rumbles through my gut at that name.

Draven Augustin.

I'd never seen it coming. Who would have known, that a tech guy like him could cause so much trouble? So much pain? I'm glad that the fucker's dead, but still, even with his body burned beyond recognition, he still haunts my life. My memories. My brothers. Our woman.

"She still hasn't talked about him." Everett's voice is low, as if somehow someone will overhear us in the moving vehicle. "Or what happened while she was with him."

I frown.

There's been so much going on this past month, between her own injuries, mine and her father's hospitalizations, that I'm sure our woman hasn't had a spare moment to think. I'm not sure what will happen when she does. What will happen when her walls come down and she has a chance to process the damage and trauma that *fucker* caused.

I just know one thing.

"We'll be there for her when she's ready. We'll keep her together, and remind her that she's *ours*." My eyes roam over the house as it comes into view.

A house that didn't feel like a home until she was in it.

It's midday, and without a single cloud in the sky, I have a clear view through a few of the windows. I can see Mrs. Claebourne passing through the dining room, chasing a flash of clothes I can only assume is one of the boys. There's no sight of Brielle, but I suppose that's best for now. Given the circumstances.

"She's going to be pissed you didn't tell her you were getting discharged." Everett laughs, somehow able to interpret my thoughts.

"Yeah, I know." I shake my head and slip from the car, smiling. "I wanted to surprise her."

"You'll be lucky if she doesn't surprise *you* with a punch to that freshly healed side of yours," he quips, falling into step behind me.

She can punch me all she wants. I'd do anything to feel her skin against mine, without the millions of wires that have been getting in the way this past month.

I'm slow to climb the front steps, and I pause at the front door, fighting back my nerves. I'm the Beast. I don't get nervous. Or, at least I didn't, before Brielle Beaumont fell into my life and destroyed everything I thought I was or ever would be.

"Breathe, Beast," Everett murmurs, and I sigh at his reminder.

A reminder I'd instructed him to give Brielle on *her* first day home.

Just breathe, Beast.

I pull in a steadying breath, and push open the door.

I'm not sure what I expected to find when I got here, but I didn't expect it to feel so…normal. Well, normal aside from the two boys racing through the living room playing tag.

"Get back here!" Rhys is laughing, his fist wagging as he chases after them.

They squeal and do their best to evade him as they round the couch, nearly tripping over one another in their haste to escape his outstretched hand.

"Boys, take it outside!" Mrs. Claebourne calls from the kitchen, and they laugh, slowing their pace.

It's not until that moment that they see me. Rhys tosses a wave in my direction, his chest heaving as if he's just run a marathon, and Samuel races up to me.

"Xander! You're home." He smiles, his body still moving as he bounces around. "Wanna play tag?"

"Sorry, Sam, but I think I should probably sit this round out." I laugh.

He shrugs, and quickly follows Noah as he runs outside. At least Sam seems to be settling in okay.

Rhys chuckles as he crosses toward us, his forehead slicked with sweat. "Those kids are fast."

"It sure looked like they were giving you a run for your money." I snicker, and he flicks me off.

"Welcome back, Xander." Mrs. Claebourne rounds into the room, the smile on her wrinkled face large. "Don't you worry, me and the boys are going to head out here in a bit. I just wanted to make sure everything was ready for your return home."

"You didn't need to do that, Mrs. Claebourne." I shake my head, and she rolls her eyes.

"Let Brielle know I'll have Sammy back on Monday. That way you four will have the weekend to relax, now that you're home." She winks at me, and my brothers are quick to look away from her knowing gaze.

I just smirk. "Thank you, Claire."

She heads toward the back door to get the boys, and I turn to Rhys, whose face is red with heat.

"Embarrassed, Rhys?" My teasing tone makes him scoff as he eyes the old woman from the corner of his eye.

"She's the closest thing any of us have had to a mom in a long time. Embarrassed doesn't begin to cover it." He shivers.

I laugh, and scan the space around us. Other than my brothers, the downstairs seems to be empty, now that Mrs. Claebourne has stepped onto the back porch.

"Someone's missing," I state, glancing around again. Her absence seems to be all the more glaring now that the house has fallen silent with the kids outside. "Where's Brielle?"

"She's upstairs in the shower," Rhys replies, his green eyes falling to Everett. "Why don't you and I help Mrs. Claebourne get the boys together?"

"Sounds like a plan to me." Everett nods.

They're quick to take off toward the back door, and I'm left standing in the foyer with my heart thumping in my chest.

Breathe, Beast.

Just breathe.

I pull in a breath, and release it as I begin climbing the stairs, my ears primed for the sound of running water. When I reach the landing, I follow the sound, passing Brielle's room and my office before I slip into my bedroom.

What is she doing in here?

Steam coils through the room, slipping out from the cracked bathroom door like a snake in search of its prey. It ensnares me and lures me in, and as I inch closer to the bathroom, the light sound of Brielle singing echoes through the room.

It's beautiful.

It's haunting.

It feels like I've glimpsed some private, unexplored piece of her, and for a moment, I wonder if I should retreat.

"Is that you, Rhys?" Her voice, so soft and uncertain, pulls me in like a siren to a passing ship.

I slip into the bathroom and seal the door shut behind me as my eyes devour our beautifully naked woman. She's standing beneath the water, rinsing her hair, and as the scent of the shampoo fills my senses, I realize why she must have come in here.

"Did you miss me, Amour?"

It's my shampoo she's using, and my body wash that's lathered her skin. That realization alone is enough to stir my cock in my jeans, but the sight of her naked body, and the gasp that leaves her lips, certainly doesn't help.

"Xander?" She swipes the water out of her eyes, and I track the movement, a wide smile creeping onto my lips as she finally spots me. "Xander! What are you doing here? Did Dr. Patel discharge you?"

I laugh as she scrambles to rinse off the suds still clinging to her body, and wave a hand. "Don't rush on my account, Amour. I'm not going anywhere."

"I was wondering where Everett ran off to. I can't believe you're finally home." She smiles and stills in her pursuit to finish rinsing, her hazel orbs locking on mine. Reaching a hand toward me, she bites her bottom lip and asks, "Join me?"

Chapter Forty-Five

Brielle

My chest rises and falls in quick succession as I watch my Beast undress. It's been far too long since I've seen him this gloriously bare, and I can't help but stare as he steps into the stall with me.

He takes my hand, the one now free of hardened plaster, and strokes a thumb over my wrist delicately.

"How does it feel?" He raises a brow and lifts those blue eyes up to meet mine.

It takes me a second to gather my scrambled thoughts, the ones that are trained solely on one *large* thing, and *not* on what he's just asked, before I can respond.

"It's, uh, still a little sore, but I'm glad to have the cast off." I smile at him sheepishly, and he chuckles.

"I'm sure my brothers were sad to learn that you no longer needed their assistance bathing." His voice is a low rumble that makes me shiver, despite the warmth of the water falling against my back.

"Yeah, they were." I giggle, and sigh, absent-mindedly reaching forward to stroke the spot where he'd been stabbed. "I was sad too, though."

"Oh?" I can hear the curiosity in his voice as I race my fingers over his puckered scar, but he doesn't press.

It would be easy to steer the conversation away from where I feel it's going. So easy in fact that I instinctively begin lowering my hand, intent on forgetting the thoughts swirling in my head, but…

I'm tired of running from it.

So, so tired.

"I-I don't like showering alone. It gives me too much time to think. Too much time to remember…" I frown and avert my gaze, no longer able to stand the sight of the injury *I* caused. "It's funny. I thought after what happened I'd never want to shower with anyone again, but—"

"Amour." He cups my chin, and tilts my head up, so I'd meet his gaze if I'd remove my eyes from the pattern in the tile. "You don't have to tell me, if you aren't ready."

My eyes lift to his, and I lean into his touch to keep myself from backing down.

"I-I want you to know. I need you to know…" My voice breaks, and I have to pull in a steadying breath before I can continue. "When, when he realized I was wearing Rhys' clothes, he, um, he cut them off…" Xander's jaw tenses as he grinds his teeth, but he doesn't tell me to stop. "H-He, he made me s-shower." I shiver, and Xander reaches behind me, intent on turning the heat up, but I stop him. "N-no hot water. Please."

He nods, and wraps an arm around me, tugging me into his chest instead. His warmth soothes some of the chills that have seeped beneath my skin, and he looks down at me, unsure. "Is this okay?"

"Yes. Thank you." I drop my head onto his chest and take a second to steady my breathing.

We stand like that for a moment, just clinging to one another as the water pours down around us. I'm fighting the urge to retreat, and find a distraction so I can forget, but I won't be able to heal if I don't get this off my chest.

"The water was so hot. It was scalding. I-I can't stand the heat anymore, I don't know why, but it's — "

"I understand," Xander gently interrupts, and smooths a hand through my hair.

"He washed me. H-he scrubbed so hard, I thought he was trying to remove my skin." I tighten my hold around Xander's middle, clinging to him as if he's a rock that can steady me in the storm. "When I was clean enough, he, um, he — " I grit my teeth as the memory of Draven's low groans of pleasure fill my ears. "He touched himself, a-and finished on me."

I can hear Xander trying to hold back a growl, but with my head against his chest, it's impossible to ignore the rumble that echoes against me. His arms tighten around me, almost to the point of pain, but I don't complain.

It keeps me grounded.

It keeps me from slipping back into the memories.

Xander doesn't say anything. He doesn't offer me the apologies I know Rhys would shower me with. He doesn't offer me a distraction like Everett would. He just stands there, holding me, while I feel everything I've been trying so hard not to feel.

I'm not sure how long we stand there, me clinging to him for dear life, and him holding onto me like I might slip away. It isn't until I hear Xander's bedroom door close that I pull back enough to look at him.

"T-Thank you. For listening." I sniffle.

He strokes my cheek and kisses my forehead. "Thank you for telling me."

Rhys and Everett's voice's carry into the bathroom, and I shrink back, unsure if I'm ready to face them. Xander, my observant Beast, notices, and is quick to call out.

"Give us a minute and we'll be out." He reaches behind me and shuts off the water. Grabbing a towel, he drapes it over my shoulders and nods his head toward the door. "I'll make sure they know to shower with you from now on, and I'll warn them about the temp, too."

"I love you." I offer him a half-smile, and he leans down, quickly pecking my lips.

"I love you. Now, get dried off, and come have some fun, hm? Mrs. Claebourne is giving us a kid-free weekend, and we are not wasting one fucking second of it."

I can't help but laugh as he climbs out of the shower and starts toward the door without bothering to dry off, or cover himself.

I guess the fun they have in mind doesn't require clothes…

I giggle, and race the towel over my body, drying off before I step toward the door. My reflection catches my attention, and I pause to scour myself in the fogged mirror.

The bruises I'd received during my time with Draven are gone. All that remains of my time in his home is a pink line along my throat, where he'd cut me with the razor blade.

That, and the memories.

I turn, continuing to scan myself and the progress I've made. The weight I'd lost in the weeks leading up to my capture has piled back on, thanks to Mrs. Claebourne and her steady stream of baked goods. My ass has filled back out, and my ribs are no longer visible beneath my skin.

I look…good.

I scoff at the thought, and know that my men would have a thousand better words to describe the way I look. Glancing toward the door, I drop my towel and start toward the bedroom.

Let's have some fucking fun.

Chapter Forty-Six

Rhys

Brielle Beaumont has given a new meaning to my nickname. I was branded Blaze in my youth out of fear of the destruction I caused, but *she* ignites me. She is the reason I burn now.

Watching her walk into the room, naked, smiling, and unashamed, makes my blood boil with need. It's exhilarating. It's sexy. It's a million things I can't fucking name because I'm too busy staring at the glorious curves of her body.

"Mrs. Claebourne took the boys?" Fuck, even her *voice* is sexy, and she's not even trying.

"She wanted the four of us to have some time together without the kids under our feet." Everett adjusts the bulge in his jeans, and straightens as she steps further into the room.

"That was nice of her," Brielle murmurs as her eyes drift to me. I'm hanging on every single move that she makes, and she smiles, noticing. "Did he wear you out?"

"W-What?" I cough, and try to pull my gaze away from her breasts, but they keep luring me in.

"Sam. He's always been really fast." She inches across the room with a grace I can't fucking comprehend, and stops just a few short feet from me.

If I reach out, I could probably grab her and toss her onto the bed... "Yeah. Yeah, he is."

She giggles, and shifts, easily closing the space between us. I'm surprised when she straddles me, her legs falling onto either side of me, but what surprises me more is the *warmth* I can feel radiating off her.

Oh, fuck me...

Her pussy presses down against the bulge in my shorts, and I shift as my need spikes.

"I hope he didn't wear you out *too* much. Xander told me that we'd all have some fun?" she whispers, glancing over her shoulder.

Like magnets, my brothers move, drawn toward her with just that simple look. Xander, already naked from their shower, climbs onto the bed behind us so he can take a spot at the head of the bed. Everett, who'd been sitting beside me, stands, and hovers behind her, his hand stroking through her wet waves.

"Your wish is our command, Flower," I whisper.

Her nose brushes against mine, and she smiles as heat creeps onto her face. "I want to take all three of you tonight."

I groan, and glance over her shoulder toward Everett, who's quickly removing his clothes.

"Well then, Flower. We'd better get you warmed up."

* * * *

Everett

Xander's room is not one that we normally keep stocked with bondage equipment and toys, so with no one willing to make a quick trip down the hall, we decide to improvise. We use a T-shirt to cover her eyes and a necktie to bind her wrists, loosely. Not that we really *need* any of it. If we told our woman not to move or open her eyes, she would, and she'd do it with that little mischievous smile on her lips.

Our woman aims to please.

We've sat her in the center of the bed, between Xander's outstretched legs. Close enough to feel his presence and warmth, but not close enough to touch him. It's making her squirm, her little body twitching with need, and I can't help but chuckle at the sight.

"Our woman is excited, brothers." My voice is a low rumble, and she flushes at my words, her teeth sinking into her lower lip.

"Mm, how I've missed this," Xander murmurs, and sits forward, no longer able to restrain himself.

He brushes her hair to the side, and bites the side of her neck, making her squeal as he moves up behind her. Hooking a hand around her throat, he collars her to his chest and buries his nose in her hair as I step toward the edge of the bed.

I've missed this, too.

I reach out and cup her breast, feeling the weight in my palm before I roll the nipple between my fingers. She moans, and presses forward as much as Xander's hold on her will allow, desperate. I give her a moment, allowing the pleasure to settle deep within her before I draw back, and smack my open palm across the opposite breast. She gasps, surprised, and I chuckle, leaning forward.

"Did you forget, pet?" I muse, and she releases a slow breath. "I was counting."

Capturing the peaked nipple of the breast I've just struck, I rub delicately, delivering pleasure before I repeat my earlier treatment to the first. She rocks in Xander's hold, groaning as I reach out to soothe away the sting.

"What did you do wrong, pet?" I ask, and her eyebrows furrow.

Panting, she replies. "I rolled my eyes."

I deliver two more slaps to each breast, light enough to ensure she doesn't welt, but hard enough that my message gets across. When I've finished, she's breathing hard, and squirming relentlessly, her body coiled tight with a need we've yet to address.

"Please," she breathes, and Rhys leans across the bed, smirking.

"Please what, Flower?" he questions mischievously.

"Touch me. Please." She wiggles, and Xander chuckles, kissing her cheek.

"We are touching you, Amour," he teases.

"M-My pussy. Please. Please," she begs, and he eyes me as he releases her throat.

He trails his hand down her neck, between her breasts, and down her stomach. She's writhing as his long fingers stroke along her skin, and she hisses out a long breath as his hand finally reaches her pelvis, where he stops.

"Fuck, please." Her head drops back against his shoulder, but it isn't until I nod my approval that he finally dips his hand between her thighs.

The Beast is giving up control.

He swirls his finger around her clit, once, twice, before his digits push inside her, making her back arch. She moans, and I swear to fuck, if a heaven for me exists, *that* will be the sound that echoes through the skies of my eternal resting place.

"I-I want to touch..." she pants out the request, and again, Xander's eyes flit to me.

I smirk, and lean forward, gently cupping her chin.

Turning her head in my direction, I ask her, "What do you say, pet?"

"Please, sir?" A smile tugs up the corner of her lips, and I groan, racing a thumb over her cheek.

"That's my good fucking girl."

Chapter Forty-Seven

Brielle

"That's my good fucking girl."

The possessiveness, the *hunger* behind his words, destroys whatever fear had clung to that phrase. It's *theirs*. Theirs to use, and no one else's.

"*Our* good fucking girl," Xander's correction sends a bolt of excitement straight to my core, where his fingers continue to push in and out of me.

I release a low breath and bite my lip as someone's hands begin working to free my wrists from the tie that binds them. It's a little sore, but it's something that's easy to ignore as my freed hand is guided around a rock-hard cock. I pull in a sharp breath and pump, twisting slightly to increase the pleasure I'm delivering.

Rhys' low moan rumbles into the room, and a quiet whimper slips from my lips in response. Giving pleasure to my men is always so *exhilarating*. Reaching out with my free hand, I search, until my hand finds an unclothed waist. Everett climbs onto the bed at my pull, and I rock my hips as Xander curls his finger inside of me, pleased as I begin stroking his brothers.

"You're so beautiful with their cocks in your hands." Xander kisses my neck, and heat creeps through my body, warming my skin as he begins stroking me in time with the movements of my wrists.

"Fuck, Xander..." I grind into his palm, desperate for a little more friction as tightness coils in my belly.

Understanding my need, he moves his thumb back up to my clit, while his fingers move in delicious curls inside me. It makes me come apart, my moans spilling into the room as my men shift to continue our night of fun.

Grinning, I lie back onto the suddenly empty bed, and I reach out, searching for them. "May I remove my blindfold, sir?"

"Not yet, pet." Everett chuckles.

I squirm, then the bed dips as someone climbs onto it near my feet. They slide up my body, and before I've had time to recover, their tongue is on my clit. I jolt and gasp, so caught off guard that I *almost* miss the feeling of someone else climbing onto the bed.

"Open your mouth, Amour." The order, accompanied with the tongue on my sensitive bundle of nerves, makes my mouth fall open with a groan.

I turn my head and open my mouth, panting as the head of Xander's cock rests against my bottom lip. I dart my tongue out, licking up the pre-cum that has collected along the tip, and that movement is enough to spur him on. He pushes into my mouth as something else, a dick, presses against my pussy. My legs spread wider, and I cry out around Xander as they push into me, my back arching as pleasure shoots through my system.

Fuck me.

Their hips move, pulling out before they push back in, and again, I scream my pleasure around Xander's cock. He groans above me, and wraps a hand through my hair, his dick rock hard as my tongue traces up his shaft.

"Fucking hell." Rhys' gritted words fall down around me as he rocks forward, spearing me. "You're so fucking tight, Flower."

His praise makes me shiver, and I roll my hips, meeting his thrusts as I suck Xander down my throat.

"Beautiful, pet." Everett's praise comes from somewhere off to the side, and I reach for him, needing him, too.

He curses, as if unable to resist, and Rhys retreats, pulling himself free of my pussy.

Wait, no.

"Patience, Amour." Xander chuckles, as he, too, retreats from me.

I frown, but as I open my mouth to complain, someone pulls off the blindfold covering my eyes. The bright light of the room makes my eyes water, and by the time my vision's cleared, my men have changed positions again.

"Are you sure you're ready for this, Flower?" Rhys asks.

He's lying on the bed beside me, cock standing at attention. Everett is hovering by the foot of the bed, his hungry gaze devouring me, while Xander kneels by the head of it.

I nod, and bite my lip before replying, "So fucking ready."

Chapter Forty-Eight

Xander

Screaming.

The sound echoes through the room around us, and I smile, my cock hardening at the pleasure laced within the noise.

"Oh, fuck. Oh fuck!" Brielle cries, lost to the pleasure my brothers are delivering.

She is fucking *breathtaking.*

Rhys lies below her, his cock driving up into her pussy, while Everett kneels behind her, taking her ass. She's knelt on all fours, her head angled up, so she can take me into her mouth, when her pleasure allows her a moment of reprieve. It's astonishing, watching our tiny woman take all three cocks at once, and I grunt as she pulls me back into her mouth hungrily.

"You're fucking beautiful, Flower." Rhys leans up, kissing her neck as he thrusts, chasing his release.

Everett groans, no doubt able to feel our brother between the thin muscle separating them, and matches his pace, making Brielle scream around me again.

She'd been uncomfortable at first. It's a lot of pressure to adjust to, but as soon as they found a pace that worked, and she relaxed, the intensity in the room spiraled as her pleasure mounted. She's come once, just from having them inside her, and I revel at the sound her wet release creates between them as they move.

"Your ass...fuck." Everett can't form a coherent thought, and as her tongue swirls around my head, her teeth biting gently into my shaft, I feel my thoughts scatter, too.

Fuck.

My head drops back, and I thrust into her lips, savoring in the warmth that grows in my balls. Already I want to spill down her throat, but I resist, waiting, *needing* her to come apart again.

I need to hear it.

I need to *feel* it.

I've been waiting for a fucking *month* for this.

"Come for us, Amour." I fist her hair, and push myself further, gagging her with my cock.

Her watering eyes lift to meet mine, and a smile curls onto her lips as her body bounces.

She's close.

"Make her fucking come," I bark the order, and Everett grunts as Rhys quickens his pace.

Her eyes flutter shut as pure ecstasy fills her, and before I know it, all four of us are falling over the edge. She screams around me, the noise vibrating my cock, and I spill down her throat as my brothers fill her with their seed. Collapsing to the bed, we all pant, sweaty, spent and so fucking *content.*

"I love you," Brielle whispers, and I move, scooping her into my arms.

Tugging her, I pull her into my side as my brothers move to take their places around her.

"I love you," all three of us reply in unison.

The room grows quiet, as we try to catch our breaths, and I smile as I kiss our woman's head.

This couldn't be any more fucking perfect.

We're going to get everything back on track. We're going to take care of her, and her family, and she's never going to want or wish for anything ever again.

Aside from our cocks.

I chuckle, and Brielle looks up at me quizzically. I just shake my head, and smooth a hand through her matted hair.

"I love you, Brielle Beaumont," I whisper, and my heart tugs at the smile that pulls onto her face.

"I'm yours, Xander Grimm," she replies, and I smile as she looks at my brothers happily. "I belong to you all. I am the Grimm Brothers'."

Epilogue

Brielle

"Open it, open it, open it!" Sammy is chanting, his hands clapping together as he jumps up and down excitedly.

I giggle and look down at the key I've been twisting around in my hand.

Is this really happening?

As if searching for confirmation, my eyes lift to each of my men, who're standing with a still-bouncing Samuel. Xander is smiling, his blue orbs glinting in the daylight, and when he catches my gaze, he nods, urging me to continue. Rhys is whooping, his own shouts of impatience mixing with Sammy's, and Everett laughs.

"Come on, pet. We're ready!" Everett calls over the noise, and I turn, excited.

After slipping my key into the lock, I twist it until an audible clunk fills the air, and push. The door swings open, and a bell jingles overhead. The familiar smell of pages rushes to greet me as I step into the warm space, and I turn, holding open the door.

"Welcome to The Gilded Rose."

A sense of pride fills me as they begin filtering into the space, and I allow myself a quiet moment to appreciate everything that's led me to this moment, as they investigate the shop. The Gilded Rose is a bookstore.

My bookstore.

It was a gift from my men, something for me, and me alone, to help occupy my time now that my plate isn't overflowing. It's somewhere for me to escape. A place for me to fulfill dreams I'd never thought possible before meeting them.

And today, it opens.

"There's a surprise for you behind the counter, Amour." Xander has stopped beside me, his arm wrapping around my waist as he tugs me further into the store. "Go look."

He urges me forward with a gentle nudge, and I smile as I walk toward the counter. The older building is downtown and is only a few blocks from their office, where they continue to run their amassed empire. It looks like it was always meant to be a bookstore, so now, as I pass row after row of the shelves I've stocked with a mixture of hard and paperbacks, I try to imagine it as it once was. A bank. The large vault that had once held money, gold bars, and safety deposit boxes is now filled with a cozy reading area. Velvet couches, plush armchairs, and a few desks line the space, urging my patrons to enjoy their time in the store. The check-out counter, where I'm headed, is situated just outside the vault, with a vintage register that's original to the bank perched at its center. It still functions, and as I slide behind the counter, I realize that the till is sitting open.

I glance toward my men, suddenly worried that I've already been robbed, but they look suspiciously calm. Surely, if something was amiss, they would have caught it on the expensive security equipment they insisted on installing before the grand opening.

What are they up to...?

I open my mouth, prepared to sling a million questions in their direction, but I pause when my eyes catch on a black jewelry box. It's sitting atop the green bills stashed within it, and as I lift it, my heart leaps into my chest. I flip the lid open, and inside is the most gorgeous diamond ring I've ever seen in my life. It steals my breath, and my watery eyes widen as someone clears their throat in front of me.

"Brielle Beaumont?" It's Rhys who's spoken, and when I find him, kneeling on the carpeted floor, my body trembles. "We know it's a lot to ask, and we aren't sure how it would work in terms of legality, but..."

"We want you to be ours. In name. In title..." Everett continues, lowering himself onto one knee. "In every way that matters."

"Marry us, Brielle." Xander's words aren't a question, and the demanding tone with which he says them seems all the more fitting for our relationship.

I laugh as he drops onto his knee, then my eyes find Sammy, who's waiting off to the side. He's nodding, and the sight of his approval pulls the reply from my lips.

"Yes. Yes." I race around the counter, and they all envelope me in their arms, cradling me between them. "In every way that matters, yes."

Cheers pour through the open door, and I tug away to see Mrs. Claebourne and Noah standing in the doorway. They rush forward with words of congratulations as Rhys slips the ring onto my finger. With shaking hands, I swipe at my warm face, and laugh as we all fall into comfortable conversation about the building and the plans for my store.

The Gilded Rose, a bookstore whose name I created to reclaim and honor my mother's memory, is a non-profit. All earnings are going to the rehabilitation center where my father is currently living. They're teaching him to exist with the deficits of his stroke, and while we hadn't been promised much improvement at the time of his discharge, our father has already made incredible progress. He's hopeful that one day, he'll be able to live on his own again. That way, he can regain guardianship of Samuel and I'll be free of the motherly responsibilities that still linger over me.

David, the hacker Beast has on staff, was able to find all the records Draven had stashed during his six years of stalking my family. With them released, we were able to take the paperwork to court and gain me temporary guardianship over Samuel while our father recovers. He was also able to move an obscene amount of cash from one of Draven's offshore accounts into a secured college fund for Sammy to use one day, if he chooses. It felt dirty at first, but now, I realize that he owes it to my family after the hell he caused us.

"Look, Flower." Rhys, still holding my hand, nods toward the door.

A woman, and three children are looking through the front windows of the shop, and after a beat, they push through the door.

"Welcome in," I call, and offer them a small wave as Mrs. Claebourne shoos the boys toward the children's section in the back.

"You've got this, Amour." Xander kisses my temple, and moves aside as the children begin rushing through the store, following after Sammy and Noah.

"We're so proud of you, pet," Everett muses.

He slides behind the counter, taking control of the register as the woman eyes the store with astonishment.

"Wow, it's beautiful in here." She gapes, and I flush.

"Thank you. Let me know if you need any help finding anything." I smile.

Everything is falling into place.

It's perfect, it's all mine, and…

I couldn't ask for anything better.

Sign up for our newsletter and find out about all our romance book releases, eBook sales and promotions, sneak peeks and FREE romance books!

Want to see more like this?
Here's a taster for you to enjoy!

Dark Sanctuary: Bound by Fear
Jayce Carter

Excerpt

"You don't look like you belong here, little fox." The man who spoke — tall, lean and dressed like a devil — was the epitome of everything Sunny had feared she'd find inside the BDSM sex club called Sanctuary.

Her breath sped, and her chest tightened as the large room shrank to nothing.

This is a horrible mistake. What was I thinking?

"Do you want to come sit with me and talk?" Devil-man asked, his lips curling into a smile below the line of his black mask. It wasn't a vicious smile, at least on the surface, but it sure felt sinister.

The desire to say no perched on her tongue, but she couldn't make it come out. She'd learned that saying no was dangerous, that it never got her what she wanted. The lesson was one that had stuck with her no matter what.

So, instead, she darted her gaze toward the crowd of people and pretended to spot someone she knew, waving in that direction.

The man stayed in his spot, letting her go, and she made a quick path for the bathroom. Once safely inside — the one place where no man would try to talk her into anything — she set her hands on the white porcelain sink and stared into the mirror.

Maybe a fox had been a stupid costume. She'd tried on a few different ones that radiated strength, but they had felt like a lie. Sunny was as soft as they came, so when she'd tried on the little white sundress, along with the fox mask that obscured her eyes, and some drawn-on whiskers, she'd known it was more *her*. Foxes were smaller than other predators, but quick and clever. She connected with that, understood it. At least, it had made sense until she'd walked into a club full of lions and tigers and dragons.

Suddenly, her fox didn't seem so clever.

One night. Prove that you don't want this anymore.

She nodded and straightened herself, pulling her shoulders back. She was here for a reason. She'd go out there, find someone to play with, and by the end of the evening, she'd know that she was done with all this nonsense. She could wake up tomorrow sure of herself, able to put this behind her. The plan helped her move forward.

The door to the bathroom opened as a woman in lingerie and a cat mask walked in, the music from outside deep and rhythmic. Her hair was blonde and beyond stunning, so pale it was nearly white. Even from behind the half-mask, her almost gray eyes shone brightly.

The woman approached, a smile across her pink lips, the color smeared as though she'd been kissing someone just before. "It's so much fun tonight, right?"

Sunny nodded despite not feeling quite so sure. "Yeah."

The woman glanced down at Sunny's wrist, at the cuff the receptionist at the door had placed there with a white ribbon. "Oh, you're new? Is this your first time?"

First? Try only. Instead of saying that, Sunny tried to smile. "Yes."

The woman stuck her hand out. "My name is Kat." She winced as soon as she said it. "I know — it's a masquerade party — it's supposed to be all anonymous. You don't have to give your name. I'm just not good at the whole secrecy thing. And *yes*, I know, Kat — cat costume — cliché, but why not, right?"

Sunny had trouble understanding Kat. She'd figured the sort of people in a place like *this* would terrify her. The men would be scowling brutes, lumbering around just looking for a victim, and the women quiet, frightened little things who cowered at everything. *That's what I was...*

Kat wasn't anything like that.

Sunny shook the offered hand, unsure how to answer, other than the fact that she wouldn't be giving her name. That would negate the entire point of her coming here on *this* night. Sunny needed to do what she'd come to do then leave — no ties threatening to trap her.

Kat chuckled, as if she could read the nerves that poured off Sunny. "Afraid of the big bad Doms? Come on — you can hang out with me. Safety in numbers, you know."

Sunny wanted to say no — it felt too much like putting herself into a life she was trying desperately to get out of. Still, having a partner next to her did feel better.

"That would be nice," Sunny admitted softly.

Kat asked her to wait a moment so she could use the restroom, then washed her hands before tucking her arm through the crook of Sunny's. It was an oddly safe feeling, as though Sunny had found a guide to this absolutely terrifying place. Sure, Kat wasn't all that intimidating, but at least Sunny wasn't alone.

They walked out, with Kat holding securely to Sunny's arm. "I love the last Saturday of the month. Something about dressing up makes everything more fun, plus it's the day we let the new folks come. It gets boring with the same old folk every weekend, and new blood is always good."

It also let Sunny move around the club with a sense of privacy, without feeling everyone was looking at her, could see her.

Sunny's gaze couldn't settle on any one thing. The bodies that moved on the dance floor, the groupings of people, the colors and costumes and activity, all fought for her attention.

And it all overwhelmed her. Sunny's world was quiet, calm. She'd worked hard to create a haven away from the craziness of everyday life.

So what was she doing *here*?

She turned her attention back to Kat, to the cuff around her wrist — identical to Sunny's except for the fact that it had a myriad of ribbons on it. Red, teal, green and yellow striped — they meant nothing to Sunny. She vaguely recalled the receptionist explaining it to her as she'd signed in, but Sunny hadn't heard any of it. Her anxiety had been far louder than rules or color coding.

"What do the ribbons mean?" Sunny asked, trying to find something to fill the silence with.

Kat held up her wrist to show the leather cuff with the colored ties. "For members, we use these to identify what people are looking for and what limits they have. We still ask of course, just to make sure, but these make it obvious right from the start. If someone hates something you love, you know it may be a bad fit before even trying. Nothing worse than a hardcore masochist falling for a Soft Dom who doesn't like to even raise their voice. Makes everyone unhappy when people don't click."

Sunny frowned when the explanation didn't make any sense to her.

Doms never care what their subs want.

However, she kept that to herself. People saw what they wanted, and Kat seemed the type to let romantic notions blind her to the truth. No doubt she'd say the Doms here were different, that they were somehow exempt from the reality Sunny had experienced before. There wasn't any reason to argue over it, so Sunny let the topic drop.

They went to one of the tables set out with coffee and snacks, and Kat filled a small plate with items for them both. "I love your costume. You sure do fit in with the whole primal and prey thing."

And *that* made the damn panic creep up again. She hadn't thought of the fox as *prey*. It was a predatory creature, just smaller than some of the others. It seemed others saw it differently.

Kat looked past the table and locked eyes with a man across the room, one who wore a black mask with horns and a smirk. He crooked his finger to call her over. She let out a sigh full of want. "I'll be right back…" She pulled away before Sunny could answer, leaving Sunny with the plate of food and no backup.

A pit started in Sunny's stomach at the way Kat had followed the demand, at the memory of how many times Sunny had done the same thing, when she'd dropped everything she'd wanted and done as she'd been told. She remembered a crooked finger, a silent demand that came a split second before anger, before violence.

It sickened her, threatened to drag her under so many worse memories.

"There you are, little fox." The devil-man from earlier came up from behind Sunny, his voice already tattooed on her brain.

She jumped, those overactive nerves of hers taking over, struggling to separate him from her past.

He's just a person. You're fine.

Right, because telling herself that made it reality... Saying it didn't make her safe, didn't do anything.

Still, she turned toward him, her shoulders hunched forward in on herself to make herself smaller. "Hello."

This is why you came. Don't chicken out now. Just one night.

He smiled, but she couldn't shake the way her brain screamed danger at her. Whether he was actually dangerous or not didn't really matter. Her body had decided, and it wasn't listening to her. It went off history, off what she knew to be true — men, especially dominant men, couldn't be trusted.

"Why don't you come on over to the couch there? We can have a talk, get to know each other. I've been watching you since you came in, and you look amazing."

Sunny tried to swallow down her fears, her doubts, but they stuck in her throat. She shifted her weight from foot to foot, unable to shake all the *'hell no'* swirling in her head. No matter how many times she reminded herself that she was here for this, she couldn't get herself to agree, to even want to agree.

He wrapped his fingers around her wrist, the one with the cuff, and tugged gently. "Come on, little sub, I don't bite too hard — at least not unless you beg."

Sickness churned in her stomach, the room becoming stifling, the air thinning.

He didn't yank, didn't tighten his fingers to the point of pain, didn't show any sort of violence or anger, yet she couldn't catch her breath. She couldn't stop herself from seeing him as the devil he had dressed as.

She followed, her body frozen and unable to fight back, to just yank and tell him no. What the hell was wrong with her?

Fear. It was what was always wrong with her, that beast she couldn't kill no matter what she did. Even when she thought she had it under control, it always reared its ugly, unwelcome head and turned her into *this*.

"I saw you the *second* you walked in," devil-man said. "You look like prey, and I am a man who likes to chase."

"I'm a man, Sunshine, and I have needs." The voice that haunted her dreams came back to her. It ran in her head as clear as if the monster from her past stood there right then, and the room blurred.

Just when she was sure she'd pass out, that she'd fall to the floor there in front of everyone, a large hand grasped devil-man's shoulder.

It wasn't violent, but it was a *clear* message of stop. "Hold up there, Jordan."

Devil-man—*Jordan?*—paused and turned toward the man who'd spoken, someone who made Sunny want to pull even farther back. This new man was tall, his body lean but strong. He wore a silver mask that covered his eyes, and his lips were pressed into a tight, unhappy line.

She did *not* want that sort of displeasure directed her way.

In fact, right then, going off with Jordan sounded like one hell of a good idea. His lean build would do far less damage than what this new man could dish out. It was like being faced with two monsters and picking the one with the smaller teeth.

"Yeah?" Jordan asked, his tone confused but not upset.

"Does she look like she wants to go with you?"

Jordan tipped his lips down, then took another slow look at Sunny, his expression lacking anger. "She didn't say no."

"Sure she did, just not with her lips. Come on now, take a better look at her."

Jordan peered down—as if just noticing the way Sunny were as far back as her arm would allow, how she leaned away and not toward him—and released her instantly. "I'm so sorry," he said, his voice softening and losing the sharpness it had before. It seemed he'd slipped from his Dom role. "Without the eyes, I have some trouble reading cues, I guess."

Silver released Jordan. "We'll talk about it later."

"Of course." Jordan looked at Sunny, somehow managing to have shrunk from the devil-man he'd been to a regular person, deflating before her eyes. "I'm really sorry, Miss. Can I get you something? A drink?"

Sunny shook her head, afraid her voice wouldn't work if she said anything. Even though he wasn't the monster he'd been moments before, her body had already thrown itself headfirst into panic.

"Why don't you go grab her something warm and sweet, Jordan, as an apology," the new man said.

Jordan nodded and rushed off, leaving Sunny there with only the man in the mask, the one who made Jordan look more like a cub. "Hey there, fox. Breathing helps, you know?"

The words struck Sunny as entirely asinine, until she realized...she wasn't breathing. She gasped in a breath, and right away her head cleared some. *Just how long was I holding it?*

"Better," the man said, then gestured toward a couch near the back, but one in view of the rest of the room. "You want to sit down before you fall down?"

I never should have come. She never should have tried to prove she was better, or that she didn't need this. Why couldn't she have stayed in the nice, safe little rut she'd spent years creating?

"I should go," Sunny said, her voice so soft that she doubted he could hear her over the music.

Yet he shook his head, that hard edge Doms wielded refusing to be argued with. Any thought that the man before her wasn't dominant fled. "Not yet. You can barely walk right now, about a mile deep into that panic attack you've got going. If I let you walk out now, you'll collapse in the parking lot if you're lucky. Do you have a friend here? Someone who can take you home?"

Again, she shook her head. There was Kat, but she wasn't really a friend. Just some girl she'd met in the bathroom.

She'd spoken to the owner, Toya, to get her invite to the event, but she wouldn't say she knew her either. Not to mention that the last thing she wanted was to talk to the one person who knew who she actually was.

Nope. She'd walked into the wolf's den all by herself, like an idiot.

"That's fine. Why don't you just take a seat? I'll sit on the other couch, give you space while you calm down. Soon as you get your wits about you, you can go. I'm not trying anything."

Sunny wanted to say no, but when she shifted her weight to her other foot, the leg gave out. It seemed her panic had taken more out of her than she'd realized, had snuck up on her without her knowing.

The man caught her, as if he'd been expecting it. "Yeah, not leaving just yet, are you? Come on." He helped her over to the couch, then pressed a hand to the back of her neck to guide her head down, to lean her forward. As soon as she did, he let her go and sat on the other couch, just as he'd said he would.

Which made her all the more suspicious. Men didn't do things to help for no good reason. They didn't give up what they wanted — *especially* Doms.

Still, she closed her eyes, focusing on the music, on the steady beat, going through the things her therapist had taught her. Focus on the now, on the scent of leather, of vanilla, of cinnamon. Pick five things she could hear — the laughter of a woman, the quiet conversation between two men, the music, the wind striking the sides of the building, the deep tone of a man — *no, not that one!*

She pulled herself together, piece by piece, until her chest eased, and she didn't feel as if she'd pass out.

Though, when she lifted her head, when the world didn't seem quite so scary, she wished she *had* passed out. Then she wouldn't have her savior in the silver mask looking at her so intently — the studying gaze of a man who knew too much already. That was perhaps the worst thing about dealing with Doms — they saw everything and were only too quick to use it to their advantage.

He held a drink, steam escaping the top. "Hot chocolate. Jordan brought it as an apology, but he figured you'd prefer if he was on the other side of the club when you looked up."

As much as she wanted to deny it, he'd been right.

He handed over the drink, and while Sunny should have thought twice about drinking it — it was from a stranger, after all — the warmth called to her. She sipped it, and the moment the sugar hit her tongue, she let out a moan. Then tried to silence it immediately. This was *not* the sort of place to make such noises.

Sure enough, the man's lips curled into a smile that made her warm in other, far less innocent places. And that reaction scared her more than anything else. She'd come here to prove she *didn't* want this, right?

She needed to sit her body down and have a long talk with it about good choices and bad choices, but that would have to wait.

"Feeling better?"

Sunny nodded, the cup in her hands like a leash for her own bravery. "Yes. Thank you."

His smile spread. "That's a pretty voice you have. It's a shame you don't use it more often."

She tried to tuck her hair behind her ear before remembering she'd braided it back.

"There you are," came another voice, one that made Sunny cringe again. A new man walked up—no, wait, two men—in metallic masks identical to the one worn by the Dom she was already with, except for the color.

The original man had a silver mask, the new one who'd spoken was in a black mask, and the third man had a golden one.

Friends? Lovers?

Sunny knew better than to ask, so she stayed quiet to figure it out on her own. Men didn't react well to a suggestion that they weren't straight, in her experience. It was like questioning their masculinity, and the last thing she wanted was to piss off these three.

"Sorry," Silver said. "I found a cornered fox who needed some rescuing."

Black lifted his gaze to Sunny, his lips sliding into a teasing smile. "So I see. Quite the prize you found yourself."

The words made her heart do that skipping-a-beat thing—not in a good way—but Silver was quick to come to her defense.

"She's jumpy, so give her some space. Jordan wasn't reading cues so well, didn't realize this fox isn't good at saying no with her words."

Gold turned his head, revealing long blond hair that had curls in it that reached nearly to his shoulder blades. He twisted as if to go explain things to Jordan, though *explain* probably meant *beat some sense into*.

Silver smacked Gold's arm. "It's fine. I told him we'd educate him later a little better—maybe we need another class on body language. He brought over some hot chocolate to help the fox get her breath back." Silver turned back to Sunny. "This is—"

Sunny shook her head. She didn't *want* to have their names. That had been her biggest rule when coming here, that no matter what happened, she could walk out, and no one would know it was her.

Well, no one except the owner, who'd marked down each person and their costume in case complaints were lodged later, but had assured her that information was confidential.

Sunny knew what happened when a person entangled their life with a Dom, when they welcomed such a person into their world—*nothing good*. Without names, without identities, Sunny could leave at the end of the night without worrying about turning into someone's property, without fear that she'd lose everything.

Again.

Silver huffed a soft laugh. "No names, huh? Well, Fox works well enough, and I suppose you can use mask colors for us. These are my friends." He gestured at the other two.

Black sat next to Silver, and Gold took a seat in the chair to the side of both couches. Strange that Sunny could feel so trapped even when none of them were right beside her.

There was something about the men that took up all the space, as if the rest of the world disappeared with them there. The music, the lights, the bodies of the other guests didn't matter anymore, not with these three surrounding her.

"So, Fox, is this your first time? Pretty sure I'd have remembered you if you were here before," Silver asked.

Sunny nodded, trying to act braver than she felt. She didn't want to look like easy prey, like something they could pick off with little work. "I just wanted to check it out."

"Doesn't seem your style," Black added, his voice not as deep, not as rough, and full of humor. "Sometimes this is all too much. No shame in being vanilla."

The tone felt condescending, as though Sunny were a prude who had never experienced anything in her life. She'd long dealt with her youthful face and sweet disposition making people think she was some naïve fawn, especially when added to her name. "I've done *this* before," she said, waving at the club to explain what she refused to say.

She'd done the whole BDSM thing. She'd experienced it all and knew exactly how badly it always turned out.

"Really?" Silver asked. Even without seeing the top half of his face, she could *feel* his lifted eyebrow.

"Yes." The word was short, but try as she might, she knew it held all the years of terror it brought back. How couldn't it?

None of them spoke for a long moment, until finally Gold answered. "And clearly it was a bad situation. Guess that explains why you're jumpy, don't it?"

Sunny curled forward more, staring into her cup as if the answer were somewhere in the swirling chocolate. Besides, not looking them in the eyes felt safer. "I don't want to talk about that."

Silver nodded. "That's fine. Not our business. A little advice, though? You need to learn to tell people no, to use that voice of yours."

Sunny opened her mouth to tell them that she'd *done* that before, and it hadn't worked. What was the point in fighting if she always lost? In her experience, 'no' only made it all the worse, only angered Doms.

Before the all-too-telling words escaped, though, she shoved them down.

What was it about these men? After her panic had ebbed, when she could think straight, she'd found herself willing to say things she knew she shouldn't. They created a wall around her, one that kept her safe from anything outside the small circle they'd formed.

And that was a dangerous thing to think and feel, especially because she should fear them more than anything else.

Will I never learn?

"You look like you feel better," Silver said. "At least, you don't look like you're about to fall down again."

Low standards.

"You want the front to call a cab? Or did you drive yourself?"

Sunny lifted her gaze toward the door, tempted by the thought of leaving. She could go home, back her little one-bedroom house, back to the quiet, the emptiness and the solitude.

And she could think about *here* more.

She returned to her dreams, the ones where she woke sweating and so close to release, with the memory of faceless men, with her wrists bound, her eyes covered and their rough, commanding voices in her ears, with her craving something she denied herself. What sort of life was that?

She'd come for one reason — to prove that *this* wasn't for her anymore. She'd get a taste, then go back to her real life understanding that the desire was just her own stupid brain playing tricks. It was nothing more than her mind wanting to relive her trauma, as if it could make sense of it if she tried again. She'd thought about it for months, looked at the website for the club and started an email to the owner over and over again. It had taken her so long to get to this point. She needed to be brave enough to face this, to prove to herself that this wasn't the life she wanted so she could finally let it go.

So Sunny shook her head. "I don't want to leave."

"Really? What is it you want then, little speechless Fox?" Silver asked.

Sunny swallowed and set her drink on the table before her trembling hands dropped it. "I want to try."

"Try what?"

"Everything."

About the Author

A mother, wife, and avid reader, Haylynn Downing grew up with an innate love of writing. In every notebook from her childhood, you can find doodles of characters and stories scribbled amongst the schoolwork that was meant to be on their pages. A resident of the Midwest, Haylynn spends her free time enjoying the ever-changing weather with her family, and creating books for her readers to enjoy. As a newly found erotica reader, it wasn't until 2020 that Haylynn discovered her passion for writing steamy, sexy romances. Now, not a day passes that new plotlines and possessive alpha males aren't taking up residence in the back of her mind, just waiting to come to life.

Haylynn loves to hear from readers. You can find her contact information, website details and author profile page at https://www.firstforromance.com

ENTWINED PUBLISHING

www.ingramcontent.com/pod-product-compliance
Lightning Source LLC
Chambersburg PA
CBHW020822260626
47169CB00003B/789